'Some flowers for me?' exclaimed Mum, and you couldn't miss that little tremor in her voice. 'Oh, but what a lovely . . .'

And then she saw the flowers and made what I can only describe as a strange, gurgling noise, the kind a sink makes when it needs unblocking. She did finally manage to murmur, 'Well, how very thoughtful of him.'

At this point, I had to put a hand over my mouth to stop myself from laughing out loud.

'Who are they from?' asked Claire casually.

'They're from Roger,' muttered Mum. 'Very unusual, aren't they?'

'Shall I put them in a vase for you, Mum?' asked Clare (nice touch).

'Well . . .' Mum hesitated. 'Perhaps later. I must admit, I don't really like plastic flowers. They seem so unnatural – and unnecessary – somehow. I mean, there are so many beautiful flowers out there. Who wants artificial ones?'

Roger, I thought, you are well and truly snookered, mate.

Also by Pete Johnson and
published by Corgi Yearling Books:

THE GHOST DOG
*Winner of the 1997 Young Telegraph/
Fully Booked Award*
'Incredibly enjoyable'
BOOKS FOR KEEPS

MY FRIEND'S A WEREWOLF
A 1998 Book Trust Selection
'Will make any reader stop and think'
THE SCHOOL LIBRARIAN

THE PHANTOM THIEF
'Another fine book from Pete Johnson'
THE SCHOOL LIBRARIAN

EYES OF THE ALIEN
'Very readable and skilfully plotted'
THE OBSERVER

THE CREEPER
*Winner of the 2001 Stockton Children's
Book of the Year Award*
'Readers will love it'
THE BOOKSELLER

THE FRIGHTENERS
'Prepare to be thoroughly spooked'
DAILY MAIL

TRAITOR
'Fast-paced and energetic'
THE BOOKSELLER

HOW TO TRAIN YOUR PARENTS
'In 12-year-old Louis, Pete Johnson has created
a boy who makes you laugh out loud'
SUNDAY TIMES

AVENGER
'It's a brilliant read'
THE SUNDAY EXPRESS

Pete Johnson

Rescuing Dad

CORGI YEARLING BOOKS

RESCUING DAD
978 0 440 86457 8 (from January 2007)
A CORGI YEARLING BOOK : 0 440 86771 1

First publication in Great Britain

PRINTING HISTORY
Corgi Yearling edition published 2001

Copyright © 2001 by Pete Johnson
Chapter head illustrations copyright © 2001 by Sarah Nyler

Set in 14/16pt Century Schoolbook by
Phoenix Typesetting, Ilkley, West Yorkshire.

Corgi Books are published by Random House Children's Books,
61–63 Uxbridge Road, London W5 5SA,
a division of The Random House Group Ltd,
in Australia by Random House Australia (Pty) Ltd,
20 Alfred Street, Milsons Point, Sydney, NSW 2061, Australia,
and in New Zealand by Random House New Zealand Ltd,
18 Poland Road, Glenfield, Auckland 10, New Zealand
and in South Africa by Random House (Pty) Ltd,
Isle of Houghton, Corner of Boundary Road & Carse O'Gowrie,
Houghton 2198, South Africa.

Printed and bound in Great Britain by
Cox & Wyman Ltd, Reading, Berkshire.

*Dedicated with special thanks to Janetta,
Linda, Robin, Bill Bloomfield, Rose Jewitt
and my two nephews, Harry and Adam*

Chapter One

It was far worse than I'd expected. I mean, I knew it was going to be bad. But my school report was nothing short of tragic.

I'll spare you the gory details. It'll only upset you. Let me just say that I've never seen so many Ds and Es on one page in my entire life.

Actually, I think I'm pretty intelligent but not when it comes to school subjects. I'm clever in other ways, though. Like I'm very observant. I notice things. I'm sure I'd make an excellent detective or private eye. I started imagining myself solving all these mysteries. I really cheered myself up.

Then I glanced down at that dire report and it was back to reality. My mum was going to take one look at this and start charging about like a rhino with a sore head. To make matters worse, Claire, my younger sister, is adored by all her teachers and her last report was more like a love letter.

If only I could lose this report or say it had been snatched away by a passing Alsatian. One boy in my class really did get his report chewed up by a gerbil. The trouble is, I don't know any gerbils. And it's too late to improve my social life now. Anyway, schools have copies of everything, don't they? They've probably got the report of Joe Miles – yes, that's me – up on the noticeboard so staff can throw darts at it.

So what can I do? I could try and alter it. The trouble is, I'd have to change just about every line. Or I could just forget to show it to my mum. That was very tempting. Only there's this silly slip your parents have to sign to prove they've read it. And anyway, my mum always knows when reports are due. It's as if she's got special antennae.

Mum arrived a few minutes later with Claire, who'd just had a music lesson. I smiled merrily at them.

'Did you have a funky day, Mum?'

'A very tiring one,' she sighed. 'Will you set the table, Joe?'

'Sure, no problemo.'

I set the table for tea quite superbly. And all

the time I was waiting for a question that never came.

It was incredible. Mum had forgotten all about my report. This was a moment for the record books. I think she must have been very flustered about her work. She shares a job at a bank with this other woman. Only the other woman has been away ill so all her work has come to Mum. This was pretty horrible for Mum, but it got me off the hook, temporarily at least.

The evening rolled on. I was sweating now, just dreading the moment when Mum's memory came rushing back.

About half past seven Dad came home. He put his case in the hall, went upstairs, got changed, read Claire a bit of a story and then came downstairs again and sank down into his chair in the sitting room.

Mum brought him in his nosh on a tray. She used to talk with him while he was eating. And Dad was always full of funny stories about the people he'd met. He'd even mimic their voices. But now he hardly says anything to her. And she usually goes back into the kitchen and listens to a discussion about the state of the economy or something equally depressing on the radio, while Dad chomps away watching television.

He chats with me though. He'll tell me about his day – he's a salesman for an office supplies firm. But much more interestingly, Dad also partly owns a shop called Fantasy Adventure. It's pretty small but absolutely crammed with old comics, books, videos, model kits and posters. And sometimes Dad will drop into the shop after work – it really is his pride and joy – and bring back something for me.

He did that night. He gave me one of the American comics which I collect. I started reading it but all the time I was waiting for my moment.

You see, I had a plan: to get Dad to read my report and sign that annoying slip thing when Mum wasn't looking. Now, of course, Dad wouldn't be thrilled by my report either. He'd sigh and suck his teeth a bit, but then he'd forget all about it, as he's nowhere near as bothered about school as my mum.

The phone rang. I was sure that it was my nan. She often rings about this time. And she'd be chatting to my mum for ages. So here was my chance. 'Dad,' I said, 'could you assassinate some people for me, please?'

He put down his mug of tea. 'Like who?'

'Like all my teachers for a start.'

Dad grinned. 'What have they done now?'

'They've all got together and cooked up this nasty report.' Then I added casually, 'Want to take a quick butcher's?'

'I think I'd better.'

I leaned forward confidingly. 'I'll warn you now, it's not a pretty sight.'

'I think I can take it.'

But Dad put the report down, a shaken man. 'This is just awful,' he pronounced.

'I know, but don't let it spoil your evening. The sun's trying to shine and there's a great football match on – well, any minute actually. So if you would just autograph the little slip here we can move on to happier topics, like who's going to win the . . .'

'Just hold on a moment. Has your mum seen this?'

'No, she was looking really hot and tired so I thought it would be best not to worry her at the moment . . .'

'How very considerate of you,' murmured Dad. But I could tell he was trying hard not to smile. 'This report says you're not working. Honest answer now. Are you working?'

'I really mean to work but when I get to school it all seems so grey and boring. And I just can't get into it somehow.'

To my surprise Dad was nodding, as if in

agreement. 'I'm very much afraid,' he said, 'you're a chip off the old block. Reading some of this is just like looking at one of my old reports. Especially that part about you spending too much time being the class clown. I had exactly the same comment.'

'So it's not really my fault. It's just something in my genes,' I cried.

'Ah, now I'm not saying that.' But then he started time-travelling again. 'You got 25% in your maths exam. Well, I can top that. I got 18% and . . .' Dad smiled at the memory, 'my mum was so worried about my stepfather seeing it that she sat down herself and changed that 18% to 48%.'

'She just sounds the best,' I said. 'I wish I could have met her.'

But she died when Dad was twelve – the same age as I am now. I think about that sometimes. Right now, though, I was thrusting that slip right in front of Dad.

'You know, we'll have to tell Mum about this eventually.'

'Yeah, sure. How about in five years' time?'

'No,' laughed Dad. 'Soon. Very soon. But maybe tonight isn't the right time.'

'Not with European football about to start.'

'That wasn't what I meant,' replied Dad.

'But still, we don't want to miss that, do we?'

Dad didn't answer but he was smiling all right. And he was actually signing my report when something truly bone-chilling happened. Mum appeared in the doorway.

It turned out that she hadn't been talking to Nan at all. Rather she'd been called by someone from work. So she wasn't in a great mood anyway.

But then she saw Dad signing away and something in her mind must have just clicked, because she blurted out, 'Joe's report is due today.' Then she came over and asked in a voice which was too polite, if you know what I mean. 'Might I be allowed to take a look at Joe's report?'

Dad did his impression of a confused hamster and said, 'Oh yes, of course. We – or rather I – thought we'd wait until you'd had a stiff drink.' He laughed. Mum didn't.

Instead she started reading, and I averted my eyes. I hate the sight of blood, especially my own. But instead, it was Dad, not me, who Mum was glaring at, which I thought was a bit odd. And she said to Dad, in this really icy tone, 'Can we have a word in private?' So they went off to the kitchen, which is where they usually go when a row is about to break out.

Other people's parents shout and throw things

when they argue. Not mine. Instead, their voices go very quiet. And all you can hear is this hissy whispering.

I was still a bit puzzled, though. I got the rotten report. Yet Mum has a go at Dad, not me. What was all that about?

At last they came back. Dad slumped down in his chair. He looked like someone who's just been told off by the headteacher.

Mum's attention turned to me. She had a distinctly hurt expression on her face. 'I'm very sorry you didn't want me to see your report. Now, I'm not going to just laugh about this with you.' She gave Dad a truly chilling glare. 'That might get me some easy popularity, but I know you're worth much more than this. And you do too, don't you?'

'Yes I do, Mum.' Always agree with your parents when they're stressed out. Basic rule of survival.

'You haven't done tonight's homework, have you?'

'Well, not yet . . .'

'I want you to go upstairs and do it now. And in future when you come in from school, you'll have a drink and then go right upstairs and do your homework. You'll be fresher and you'll get it over with, won't you?'

I nodded solemnly.

'Now, off you go.'

I took one lingering look at the European football and at my dad.

He never said a word, just winked at me.

Chapter Two

One week later my mum and dad were waiting for me when I got back from school.

That gave me a shock I can tell you. Dad was never home this early. Immediately I thought, I'm in trouble again. But then they both gave me these really big, welcoming smiles as if I'd just got back from a war or something. I nearly turned round to see if someone had crept in behind me. My parents hadn't smiled at me this much since the day I was born.

Then Dad asked me if I'd had a good day at school. And Mum bustled around getting me a drink and a massive slice of chocolate cake. They know I'm broke so they can't want to borrow money, I thought.

I sniffed. I could smell cooking. 'Yes, we've got roast chicken for later,' said Mum.

Now, we only ever have meals like that on

Sundays or at Christmas. Never on a Wednesday.

'You're not trying to butter me up before telling me I'm being packed off to boarding school or borstal or the local zoo or . . . ?'

'Now, stop being silly and come into the sitting room,' said Mum.

Claire was already there, sitting on the sofa, taking little, delicate sips of milk. Mum plonked down beside her, then said, 'Come and sit next to me, Joe.'

So I joined the team on the sofa, wondering if Dad was going to squash beside us too. But he didn't. And he didn't sit in his usual chair either. Instead, he hovered by the door as if he was waiting for someone to invite him inside.

I decided my dad had got promotion and it meant we were going to have to move away. That's why Mum and Dad were being so creepy to us. But then I watched Dad again. He certainly didn't look like someone who's just got promoted.

All at once this icy feeling ran through my stomach and I thought, I know what you're going to tell us. Well, it wasn't any big deal. It had happened to practically everyone in my class, including Lee, my best mate.

Parents break up: that's what most of them do these days. Only not mine. I didn't want it happening to my mum and dad. I really didn't. But now Mum was saying in this slow, careful voice, like a teacher trying to explain a particularly difficult maths problem, 'Lately your dad and I haven't been very happy together. I wonder if you've noticed anything?'

Parents really insult your intelligence sometimes, don't they? Of course I'd noticed. How could I not notice scenes like . . . well, the other morning I was munching my breakfast in the kitchen and Mum was putting the toast under the grill, when Dad appeared in the doorway and muttered, 'So how does one get a button sewn onto a shirt in this place?'

For a moment I thought Mum was going to fling one of those pieces of toast at him. But she didn't. Instead, she turned round very slowly and said, in a very tight, controlled voice, 'Well, you've got three choices, haven't you. You can either sew it on yourself, get one of your many fans at work to sew it on for you, or you can throw the shirt away and buy another one. The choice is yours.'

Without another word Dad shuffled off, while Mum stood there shaking for a moment. I'm not often quiet. But I decided this had better be one of my rare, silent moments. So I just carried on chomping.

I never said a word about that early-morning encounter. But of course I remembered it.

Here's something else I'd noticed. Dad never seemed to make Mum laugh any more. In the past he had. In fact, Mum would often explode with laughter at something he'd said. Now they were hardly ever in the same room for longer than about seven seconds. Except sometimes Mum would go into the sitting room and start picking up shoes and patting cushions and saying, 'Someone has to make this a pleasant place to live.' While Dad would just grit his teeth and rustle his newspaper about.

Anyway, there was silence now while Mum waited for us to answer her daft question. In the end I just nodded. Claire didn't say a word.

'Now, your dad and I have been together for a long time.' Mum's voice shook slightly when she said that. But then she returned to her speaking clock tone. 'But now we need to look afresh about where we're going next, and to do that, we need some space.'

I found that a bit puzzling as they were hardly ever in the house together anyhow. Surely they had plenty of space already.

'So we are separating,' announced Mum.

'Is Dad moving out?' I asked at once.

'Yes, I am.' Dad spoke from the other end of the

room and already it seemed as if he was floating away from us.

'But can't you separate in the same house?' asked Claire, suddenly coming to life. 'That's what Anne Macey's parents did. They each had two rooms . . .'

'No, I'm leaving,' said Dad.

'But you will come back?' called Claire.

At the same time I was asking, 'But you're not divorcing?'

'No, we're not divorcing,' said Mum. 'Your dad and I just need to see where our relationship is going.'

How could my parents split up over something so vague as to where their relationship was going? What exactly did that mean anyhow?

And then my spine gave a little shiver. That stunt I'd pulled last week about my school report had certainly set Mum and Dad against each other. Was that partly to blame for this happening now? No, it was just a weird coincidence, that's all.

Still, the idea kept gnawing away at me.

'So you will have two houses to visit,' continued Mum. 'But the important thing to remember is that we both care about you as much as before. And we'll still be a family too. That's why I've prepared this special meal for us to enjoy together.'

'A kind of Last Supper,' I quipped.

Dad gave a strange kind of laugh. Mum patted my hand and squeezed Claire's too. 'I know you both like roast chicken. In fact it's a top favourite, isn't it?'

At this point Claire began to cry, but ever so politely and quietly. Mum put her arm around her and then announced in a very shaky voice, 'Right, I think it's time to eat now.'

And she really had pulled out all the stops with that meal. Normally Mum just whacks the vegetables and potatoes onto your plate. But today they were all in big, posh dishes, the kind we only get out at Christmas. And the gravy was in a special gravy boat too. Even the knives and forks weren't our usual ones. Mum had prepared masses of food – enough for seconds and thirds.

I don't think any of us wanted the meal to be silent. So we all kept the conversation going. Even so, I was massively relieved when the meal was over. It seemed to have lasted for two thousand years.

I helped Mum stack up everything in the dishwasher, then escaped for a while and went out on my bike. I cycled around for ages, thinking about it all.

When I got back I heard Mum upstairs with Claire who was saying, 'But why are you and

Dad separating? I still don't understand.'

For a horrible moment I thought Dad must have gone, slipped away. But then I went into the sitting room and there he was, sunk in his chair as usual. My dad must have spent half his life lately sitting in that chair. Maybe now you're picturing him as someone really ancient and wrinkly. The weird thing is, he's pretty young-looking as dads go. He's also very tall, hasn't got a paunch yet and has still got all his own black naturally curly hair.

No, the reason my dad sits in his chair so much is that he just loves watching videos of old sci-fi shows.

He's got an amazing collection too. Shelves and shelves of them in the little room upstairs he calls his study. Although, really it's just a store-house for all my dad's things now. There's one whole shelf of *Star Trek* and another of *Dr Who*, one of which Dad was looking at now. He switched the video off when I sat down.

My dad always looks as if he's in a bit of a dream. But tonight even more so – and kind of dazed too.

'Ah, Joe, there you are,' he said. He gave me this apologetic smile. 'Been out on your bike again?'

'That's right.'

He sank deeper into his chair. 'Anything you want to ask me at all?' He was trying to talk in his usual cheerful voice but not quite succeeding. I stared at my feet for a long moment, then blurted out, 'Well, there was one thing. What happened last week about my report? Did that have anything to do with you and Mum breaking up?'

'Not a thing,' replied Dad at once.

'Only my next report will be better, I promise. Well, it can only improve, can't it?' Then I added, 'Mum was pretty mad about my report.'

Dad shook his head, then said in this very low voice he only ever uses when he's annoyed about something, 'Your mother's been mad with me for a long while, and about so many things.'

That made it seem as if Mum was chucking Dad out, which I'd suspected already. So when would Dad leave? I wanted to ask him. And yet, in a way I didn't. Asking him seemed to make all this mess more real somehow.

And right now I just wanted it all to go away. So instead I didn't say anything for a few moments, neither did Dad. I glanced down at the video case on the table.

'I know that face. Jon Pertwee, the third Dr Who, 1969–74.'

Dad looked up. He was smiling now. 'Very

good and this episode has never been on tape before. It only came into the shop yesterday.'

'But you've seen it before?' I asked.

'Yes, I remember watching it with my mother. It scared me – but it scared her too. And at the end she leapt up and said, "I think we need a cup of tea to recover from all that."' He laughed. 'Of course, it will probably seem quite tame to you now – if you'd like to see it.'

'Of course I would.'

To be honest it was a bit creaky. I still liked it though. Dad and I watched two whole episodes and had a friendly argument about who was the best Dr Who. (He voted for Jon Pertwee, I picked Tom Baker.)

And at the back of my mind I was thinking it would probably take Dad weeks to find somewhere to live. He could be here for yonks yet. And maybe by then, he and Mum would have worked out where their relationship was going and he wouldn't need to leave at all.

In fact, my dad left the very next day.

Chapter Three

If our school heating hadn't suddenly broken down, Claire and I would never have seen him leaving home. We'd have come back at the normal time to discover our home was now missing – one dad. I wouldn't have liked that at all. But seeing him pack all his cases into the car was thirty million times worse.

I stood at the top of the road, watching Dad lugging out all those cases, just as he did when we were setting off on holiday. And I was so astonished I didn't know what to do. This had just happened so incredibly quickly.

All at once I sprinted towards him. 'Dad, what are you doing?' I yelled, which must rank as one of the stupidest questions of the decade. What did I expect him to say? *I'm playing this new game called how many cases can you fit into one car. It's great fun.*

But Dad didn't seem as if he was having great fun. Actually, I'd never seen him look so tired and weary. 'Hello, son,' he said. Then his voice went all quiet. 'We thought it would be best if I just slipped away.'

'But where are you going?' I exclaimed.

'One of my customers at Fantasy Adventure is going abroad for a year. He's letting me rent his house. And it's not far away at all. Your mother's got the address.'

Mum appeared in the doorway. It was hard to tell who looked more washed-out, she or Dad. 'You're very early, Joe.'

'The heating broke down so they let us push off after lunch,' I began. I was interrupted by a voice, more like a kind of great howl. It was Claire, letting us know she'd just seen what was happening and was not very pleased about it. She charged towards us at a speed a mad bull would have envied. Tears were spurting down her face.

'No, no, no!' she cried. 'You're not going, Dad. I won't let you.' Then taking everyone by surprise she grabbed the one bag which hadn't been packed away in the car and tore up the stairs with it. And considering it must have been quite heavy, Claire moved amazingly fast. The next thing we knew, she'd locked her bedroom door.

Both Mum and Dad went upstairs and spoke as sweetly and coaxingly as they could, but she wasn't opening that door.

Now they were in a right fix. 'This isn't like her,' they said. Then they went into the kitchen and, just for a change, had a row. I couldn't help over-hearing it as I had my ear to the door at the time.

Mum was whispering. 'This is just what I didn't want to happen. I told you to leave this morning.'

'But I had a lot to do, and how was I to know the school heating would break down?' muttered Dad.

I won't write down any more of their argument because it really wasn't very interesting. They were just blaming each other and going round and round in circles. But then I heard my name mentioned and I hopped away from the door, just before it opened.

Mum said, 'Joe, love, will you have a word with your sister and get her to open the door? She might listen to you.'

Personally I doubted it, because Claire and I weren't close. We'd got on really well once. In fact, she was like my small shadow, following me everywhere. But lately we'd drifted apart.

She's a bit too perfect for my taste. And to be

honest, a bit too clever as well. You see, we attend the same middle school and I'm always being compared to her.

The trouble is, I'm extremely average. And even if I tried I'd only get C for everything, except for maths (I'm on the borderline of complete thicko where that's concerned.) While Claire is a bit of a whizz at maths and at just about everything else. That bugs me sometimes.

But anyway, I trudged up the stairs and knocked on the door. To be honest, I was kind of intrigued as Claire never usually causes a fuss about anything.

'Are you alone?' she asked.

'Yeah, it's just me and the Invisible Man,' I replied.

And then I was gazing at this pale, red-eyed figure who locked the door quickly behind me. She doesn't even look anything like me. She's small and kind of fragile-looking with dark hair like Dad, while I'm tall, with a permanently, cheeky expression on my face (so people tell me anyhow) and hair as blond and fluffy as a day-old chick's.

I prowled around her bedroom. I hadn't been in here – except to throw something at my sister or to tell her tea was ready – for ages.

'I won't let him have it you know,' she cried.

She was huddled up on the bed, Dad's bag beside her. 'I'll stay up here for weeks if I have to – perhaps you can bring me in some food. But I'm not letting him have this bag, ever.'

'Claire . . .' How could I say this without sounding snide? 'Dad can just take off without this bag. There's nothing vital to his life in it.'

'What is inside it?' she asked.

I unzipped the case and out fell a pile of shirts.

'And look at the way he's packed them,' said Claire. 'They'll get all creased like that.' And she proceeded to fold up Dad's shirts properly. 'Honestly, he's hopeless.' She'd heard Mum say that about Dad. And Claire said it just as Mum used to, really affectionately, almost proudly.

'Is it just shirts in there?' I asked.

'No. There are some *Star Trek* videos, too.'

'Now, they are vital to Dad's life,' I grinned.

On Claire's bedside table I noticed a pile of photographs. On the top was a snap of the four of us on a picnic. It rained practically the whole time. But it was still good fun. In the picture, Dad and Mum were both laughing, while Claire was smiling sweetly and I was pulling a stupid face, as usual.

'Look at them,' demanded Claire. 'They were so happy then. Why aren't they happy now?'

'That's parents for you,' I replied. 'Totally

29

useless and irresponsible. But they're not getting a divorce though, they're just having a bit of a break from each other.'

'What if Dad doesn't come back?'

'He will,' I said. 'We'll make sure of it.'

A little gleam came into Claire's eyes. 'Yes we will, and we won't tell anyone at school what's happened either.'

'Well, I might just tell Lee, but no-one else. It's none of their business anyway.'

Then we heard a very gentle tap on the door. 'Claire?' called Mum.

'I'm not ready yet,' whispered Claire to me.

'Well, it'll do them good to wait a bit longer after all the trouble they've caused.' So I yelled, 'Claire's not ready yet.'

'All right, no rush,' replied Mum, in such a meek un-Mum-like voice, Claire and I both burst out laughing.

A few minutes later I opened the door and announced in my best doctor's receptionist voice, 'Claire will see you both now.'

Mum went in first and had a chat with Claire. Then Dad spoke to her for ages.

Later Mum said the dreaded word, 'home-work,' to me. So I was sitting at my desk, thinking that homework was a total waste of my talents and how I'd probably learn more off the Internet anyway, when Dad put his head round the door.

He was carrying the bag which Claire had taken. 'Claire's asleep,' he whispered. 'So I think I'll set off now.'

'All right, Dad.'

'Now, I'm not far away. And your mother's got my new address and phone number.' He came over to me. If this had been an American TV series he'd have given me a massive hug. But we're not big on hugs in my family. So instead he just smiled at me and ruffled my hair. 'I'll be in touch,' he said.

'I'll be in touch.' That's what a very casual acquaintance or someone you met on holiday might say. But not your dad.

He picked up his bag and crept downstairs. I never heard him say goodbye to my mum. The next sound I heard was the door clicking shut.

Then I stood at the window and watched him drive away.

Chapter Four

The very next day, Dad rang up just before tea. I heard Mum muttering to herself, 'He would call when I'm dishing up.' But he didn't talk for long: just told Claire and me that he'd moved into his new abode and that was it, really.

It was good chatting to him but dead weird, too. I started wondering what he'd do after he rang off. I bet he wouldn't cook himself anything much. He'd probably just heat up some beans. Yeah, I could see him eating those beans all on his own, then watching videos for about five hours.

And even though Dad never did much at home, the house seemed odd without him. I sort of missed seeing his car in the driveway and his case in the hall. Wherever I looked there was a space now.

I wasn't in the mood for homework either (just

for a change), so as soon as I could I slipped over to Lee's house and told him everything I've told you. We were in this small shed at the bottom of the garden because Lee's mum had some neighbours round.

I've got lots of friends (I think) but only one mate – by which I mean someone I can totally trust.

Lee is that lucky person.

To my surprise he was pretty impressed with the way my folks had handled things.

'It was good they both tried to tell you properly about separating . . . and having that meal afterwards. Now, that shows real class.'

'I suppose,' I said doubtfully.

'Compared to my parents, it does,' he said.

'That's true. For ages you didn't even know your dad had gone, did you?'

'Well, I noticed he wasn't in the house. But my mum kept telling me he was away at a conference. I did think this conference was going on for a heck of a long time. But when you're young you just believe whatever rubbish they tell you. I mean, I believed in Father Christmas until I was about eight.'

'Aaah. Your mum told you in the end though, didn't she?'

'About Father Christmas?'

33

'You're so funny. No, your dad.'

'Yeah, one night I was just going off to sleep when she pops her head round the door and shouts, "I think it's time you knew the truth. Your father's not going to be living with us any more."'

'What did you say to that?' I asked.

'Not much, as I was half asleep at the time. I do remember asking Mum where exactly Dad had gone.'

'A reasonable question.'

'She just stuttered for a minute and said, "We don't need him here any more, poppet."'

'Poppet!' I laughed.

'She still calls me poppet now sometimes,' said Lee. 'It's got that it's not even embarrassing any more.'

'So when did you find out about your dad and Eileen?'

'I didn't know Dad was messing about with her until weeks later. And then I only heard Mum's side of it. I didn't see Dad for yonks.'

I'd heard all this story before but now it seemed to have a fresh ghastliness. I leaned forward. 'You see your dad all the time now though.'

'Sure, he's always taking me off somewhere at the weekends.'

'Alton Towers last weekend, wasn't it?'

'That's right. It's just,' he lowered his voice a little, 'she always has to come along too.'

'That's a bit naff.'

'Oh, she's OK,' went on Lee. 'I mean, the first time I met her I was all set to hate her. She was the woman who'd wrecked my happy home, all that stuff. But then I saw this little blonde girl in a pink sweatshirt with frogs all over it and looking so nervous . . . What she's doing with my dad I do not know. He's about twenty years older than her for a start. Not that he acts his age any more. He wears this baseball cap now and,' he wrinkled up his nose, 'he's always holding hands with her.'

'You never told me that.'

'Well, I was hoping they'd grow out of it. But they haven't. They make me feel like a right gooseberry, I can tell you.' Then he started to laugh. And I laughed too. But inside I was shuddering. I'd really hate to see my dad start acting like that.

'They kiss in front of me too, you know.'

'Yuk!'

'They don't do it regularly but they have done it. The first time it happened I thought I was going to be sick all over them. But . . .' He shrugged his shoulders. 'I'm pretty mellow about it now.' Then he added, 'Did I tell you my mum's seeing someone too?'

'No,' I gasped.

'This guy called Marti. She says he's just a friend, but every time he rings up she gets all giggly and excited.'

'I can't imagine your mum like that.'

'I know. They're normal for years and years and then one day they just suddenly change.'

'Now you're scaring me,' I said. And he was.

'Oh no,' said Lee quickly. 'What's happening to your parents is quite different.'

'Is it?'

'Of course it is. Your parents are only separating. Well, Tim Byrne's parents did that.'

'Did they?'

'Yeah, when we were in Year Six. And they spouted the same gush as yours about needing space to find out where their relationship was going. I reckon parents just get bored and fancy a change for a while.'

'But his relics are back together now, aren't they?' I asked.

'Oh yeah, they just split up for about two months. I reckon your parents will take about that long before they're back together. It only gets tricky when you have an Eileen on the scene. Then it can get pretty nasty. But your mum and dad are just having a little holiday from each other. So don't worry about it, all right.'

'All right,' I smiled.

'And think of all the good things that are going to happen to you.'

Now I looked puzzled.

'All the presents,' cried Lee. 'Tim Byrne said the present count rises dramatically when your parents separate, because they each try to out-do each other. So you get more presents and better quality ones too.' He grinned. 'Actually, Tim was quite annoyed his parents got back together just before his birthday. He felt he'd really missed out.'

'So I'd better put my orders in now,' I laughed.

'That's right. You've got it made really. You're going to have all these extra presents over the next few weeks – yet you know your parents' break-up is only temporary. What could be better?'

Good old Lee. I knew he'd cheer me up.

Chapter Five

On Sunday afternoon Claire and I heard Dad's key in the lock and Claire just raced downstairs and dived straight into Dad's arms. I don't go in for that sort of mushy behaviour myself (far too cool), but I grinned at Dad in a very pleased sort of way and said, 'Well look, it's my old flesh and blood come to take me to the movies.'

Dad was wearing his newish black jeans and a dark blue shirt which needed a bit of an iron, but otherwise he looked pretty smart. There was one strange thing though. Dad shuffled about in the hallway like a visitor. He looked lost in his own house.

Then Mum popped up and she and Dad began this mind-numbing conversation. Here's a quick sample:

Dad: 'Ah, hello, how are you?'

Mum: 'Still busy at work. But fine. How are you?'

Dad: 'Absolutely fine.' (Bit of a pause) 'Still, the weather's improved, hasn't it?'

Mum: 'Yes, it should stay nice.'

If I write down any more you'll be asleep. But you get the idea. They were so excruciatingly polite I began to wonder if they'd ever actually met before.

Finally, Mum said, 'I've left all your post in the kitchen. I hope that's all right.'

Dad did his impression of a nodding-dog and followed Mum into the kitchen, while Claire and I were supposed to be getting ready.

'Now, we must be very slow,' said Claire. 'Give them lots of time together.' She sighed. 'Mum's missed Dad so much, you know.'

Claire had been studying Mum really closely since Dad had gone, determined to see signs of Mum's broken heart. Every evening Claire would nudge me and whisper, 'Look at Mum's face now. She's so unhappy.'

So I'd glance across at Mum and at first she looked exactly the same to me. But then I figured, maybe she was looking a bit wistful. Then again, she might just have had indigestion.

I did notice how incredibly nice Mum was to

us both. Nothing was too much trouble and she never ever got cross. Not even when one of her best plates accidentally jumped out of my hand and smashed spectacularly. Mum just smiled and said, 'I broke a plate yesterday too. It must be catching.'

Anyway, when Claire and I finally came downstairs, Mum and Dad weren't swooning in each other's arms as Claire had half-expected (I hadn't). Instead, Mum was vigorously cleaning the sink, while Dad was standing up reading his post. And neither of them was saying a word to each other. They'd obviously used up all that polite chatter. Still, I told myself, they weren't rowing. That was something.

And Mum did wave us off, saying she was sure we'd have a good time and something else which I heard, but then completely forgot . . . unfortunately.

The film we saw was about a talking cat. Have you seen it? It's not bad if you're in the mood for a movie about a wise-cracking cat who also stops a bank robbery. I wish the cat hadn't sung though, (and certainly not 'Purrfect Day').

Throughout the film, Dad lavished ice-cream, popcorn and chocolates on us. When the film finished he asked if we fancied anything to eat. Of course Claire and I both said 'Yes.' (Claire may look sweet and frail but she can pack away her food with the best of them.)

I suggested a carvery where you can eat as much as you pile onto your plate. Only, Claire and I heaped so much on, food started firing off the plates in all directions as we walked back to our table. Dad was in fits watching us.

Then, after Claire and I had been munching away for a while, Dad said, 'I just want you both to know that although I'm not at home all the time, I'm only a telephone call away and I'll always be here for you.' His voice actually wobbled when he said 'always'.

'Oh Dad, we really miss you.' Claire's voice had turned distinctly wobbly too.

That's why I rushed in. 'Look, what is all this? You'll be back before we know it, won't you?'

Dad didn't say that yes, he would. But he didn't say no, either. So that was pretty hopeful.

At the car he had presents for us. (Lee was spot on about that.) He'd wrapped them up like Christmas presents too. There was a computer game for me and a pony book for Claire.

I was pleased with my gift: Claire wasn't so thrilled with hers.

'You've got that book already, haven't you?' said Dad.

'Well, actually I have,' replied Claire sadly. 'It

doesn't matter though. It's always handy to have a spare.'

'No, I'll get you something else. What would you like?'

Then, quick as a flash, Claire said, 'Actually, there are some new shoes I'd really, really like.'

Now, I'd already heard her ask Mum for those shoes. But Mum always likes to make you wait for things; she thinks it's good for your soul or something. So she had said, 'Well, maybe later in the month, love.'

Claire was bitterly disappointed. She'd wanted them right then. Even so, I was a bit shocked to hear her ask Dad for them. I think she was too, because she turned bright red. I also couldn't help observing that her shoes would cost a lot more than my computer game. Did that mean I'd get a second present? I was tacky enough to think that, but not quite tacky enough to say it aloud.

Anyway, we managed to get to the shoe shop just before closing time. Claire found her shoes instantly. I joined Dad in saying how nice they looked, although I can't remember anything about them now, not even the colour.

But I do remember Claire going bright red again when Dad was buying the shoes for her. 'You think I'm awful, don't you?' she murmured in a small voice to me.

'Shameless.' But then I went on, 'You're exploiting a situation, but why shouldn't you? We didn't cause it, did we? We're its victims really.'

'That's right. We are,' agreed Claire. 'And I've wanted those shoes for so long.'

At home Mum was waiting for us at the door. 'I was afraid you'd got lost.' She gave a funny kind of laugh. 'I thought the film finished at a quarter to four. So I hope the meal isn't spoilt. It's one of your favourites.'

Then Mum, noticing our faces asked, 'You haven't eaten already, have you?'

'We have, actually,' confessed Claire.

'Oh well, never mind. Not to worry,' continued Mum in this bright, high-pitched voice. Then Mum spied our presents. And she looked so shocked and so horrified I wanted to just throw my computer game into the road or something. I felt I'd really let her down. So did Claire who was practically in tears. But it was Dad she was eyeballing.

'I didn't know you were buying the children gifts as well. I hadn't realized we were doing that.'

Every word had icicles on it.

Dad didn't reply, just stared at her.

'And perhaps next time, you'll let me know if

43

you're taking the children out to eat!' she snapped.

'I'll fill out a form in triplicate if you wish,' muttered Dad.

Can you believe it? They were starting to fight. Well, this just wasn't fair. I mean, the whole point of them being apart was to help them to get on better. If they were going to row, they might just as well live together again.

'I've spent a lot of time preparing this meal,' went on Mum, in full flow now. 'All I ask from you is a little consideration. If you'd only thought to give me a quick call on your mobile.'

But she was talking to Dad's back. He was already marching towards the car muttering, 'I just wanted to give the children a good time.'

He was so stressed out, he nearly drove off without even saying goodbye to Claire and me. Then he quickly recovered and was his usual self again. 'Now don't worry. I shall return and see you both soon.'

But that was too vague for me.

'When exactly will Dad Cabs be calling again?' I asked.

He grinned. 'Next Sunday. Same time. Same place. And we'll go wherever you want, all right? You can choose.'

'Well, thanks for a really great time,' I said.

'We'll miss you,' added Claire.

But we whispered those last two things to Dad, as Mum was still hovering in the doorway.

Claire's lip was trembling.

'It's better if you don't cry,' I hissed. 'It'll only get Mum more annoyed.'

Claire gave a massive sniff, then said firmly, 'I'm not crying.'

'And this meal Mum's made,' I continued, 'we're going to have to eat some of it.'

Claire nodded bravely. 'All right.'

'Well, just eat what you want,' said Mum, when we told her. 'I won't be offended if you leave any.'

So we tucked in again. It wasn't that difficult to eat, as it was one of my favourite meals and my stomach's like a tank anyway.

'I expect you've had a very enjoyable afternoon,' said Mum.

I was about to say 'Yes, we have,' but something in Mum's tone stopped me. 'The film was OK but very corny.'

Claire caught on fast. 'And not as funny as we'd expected.'

I knew that was a lie but it was in a very good cause, as Mum was starting to lighten up now. And that's what happens when your parents separate. You turn into a double agent: telling your dad you had a great day, but telling your mum something completely different. It's all to do with keeping the peace – and making sure both your parents stay happy with you.

As for those presents: well, Mum seemed to forget about my computer game, but she kept glancing at Claire's new shoes. She didn't say anything but we could tell she didn't approve at all.

So after tea, Claire put the shoes in the back of her cupboard and that's where they stayed.

'If I wear these shoes Mum will only get the hump,' said Claire. 'And I hate them now anyway.'

'You hate them?' I exclaimed.

'Yes, because they're a symbol of how greedy and scheming I've become.'

I just laughed at that.

But those shoes went on skulking in the back of Claire's wardrobe, unworn and unloved. I wouldn't be a bit surprised if they're still in there now.

Chapter Six

The following Sunday, Dad turned up again to take Claire and me out. We opted to go to the fair. We went on every ride and I won – prepare to be impressed – two goldfish. It was pretty good. But it also felt a bit forced. We were all trying too hard to enjoy ourselves, especially Dad.

And he gave us some more presents, which would have been great if they hadn't felt like consolation prizes: *I'm sorry you haven't got your dad living with you any more but have another computer game to make up for it.*

Then, of course, Claire and I had to get our presents past Mum. This was a bit like going through customs. But Mum only twitched a little when she saw our latest offerings. And she thanked Dad for bringing us back in time for tea.

She and Dad had gone back to being very

polite with each other again. I think they both felt bad about rowing last week.

Dad asked if he could pick up some shirts from the bedroom (that's what he called it: not our old bedroom, but the bedroom). And Mum said, 'But of course.'

I followed Dad upstairs. I didn't want him taking too much more stuff away. But in fact I found him staring at the walls. Mum had just finished painting them yellow which can't have been Dad's favourite colour as he was looking pretty narked.

'I'm not wild about yellow either,' I began. 'I prefer black myself. You can't go wrong with black, can you?'

Dad didn't answer, just muttered through clenched teeth, 'Well, it hasn't taken her long.'

He obviously thought he should have been consulted about any colour change to the bedroom. To be fair, I could see his point.

Then Dad let out this cry as if he'd just stubbed his toe. Actually, he was pointing at a message over the bed. It said, 'THE REST OF YOUR LIFE STARTS NOW.'

'How long has that been up there?'

'A few days,' I said, vaguely. 'There's another one up in the kitchen.'

'Is there indeed!' cried Dad.

Now I thought those messages were a bit naff too, but Dad was practically frothing at the mouth and acting as if Mum had just joined a crazy sect.

He flung some shirts into a bag. Then he marched downstairs again to be greeted by Mum smiling nervously at him and saying, 'We're just about to eat and you'd be very welcome to join us.'

Claire and I exchanged pleased looks. Mum was obviously missing Dad a lot and this was her way of trying to reel him back in. At this rate the two of them would be back under one roof in no time.

But to my total horror Dad replied in a brusque, tetchy voice, 'No, no, I can't. I've got to get back.'

And this was especially shocking because Dad is never rude to anyone, ever.

Without another word Mum shot into the kitchen. To call the atmosphere tense now would be a massive understatement. Trying to cheer things up, I said, 'Dad, my eating habits have dramatically improved. I only dribble when I'm excited now. And it's not every day you have the chance to party with a guy who's just won two goldfish. So go on, stay, please.'

'I'm sorry, Joe. I really can't,' muttered Dad and left.

Meanwhile, Mum was banging about in the kitchen. I wondered if I should tell her that Dad was cross about her painting the bedroom walls yellow and sticking up messages. But in the end I decided it was best to stay out of it.

The next Sunday, as soon as Dad's car pulled up, Mum grabbed some files from work and charged up the stairs. She shut her bedroom door with a bit of a bang and stayed there.

Dad was supposed to be spending some time in the house with us. But he quickly changed his mind and decided to take us for a drive instead.

He said to Claire, 'Sweetheart, tell your mother we're going out, will you?'

After she'd gone, I asked in a very friendly way, 'Dad, wouldn't it have been better if you'd told Mum yourself?'

You see, I wanted Mum and Dad to keep talking, even if it was only about the weather. And I certainly didn't see why Claire and I should have to start delivering messages between them.

But Dad just gave this rather grim laugh and changed the subject. Later when I mentioned Mum's name again, he looked blank for a couple of seconds, then talked about something completely different.

Mum was just as bad. When we returned from

the drive – Dad didn't come in this time – she fussed about making us tea. But she never once referred to our afternoon with Dad. She didn't even ask if we'd had a good time. She just behaved as if those past few hours had never happened.

Crazy or what?

What I really hated, though, was when Dad rang up in the week and Mum answered, because she'd never say, 'Oh hello, how are you, isn't it cold tonight?' as she would if, say, Lee had phoned. She'd never utter one syllable to my dad. She'd just announce in this drab, flat voice, 'Joe, it's for you.'

Mum and Dad weren't just living in two different houses now, but two different realities, where the other one never ever existed.

I tell you, this not-talking lark really got me down. In the end the person who sorted me out was Lee. He said that provided your mum and dad aren't messing about with anyone else, you'll be fine. They're just having a massive sulk and neither wants to be the one to crack first.

I must have still looked doubtful, because he went on, 'I had a word with Tim Byrne. I was very subtle and I didn't bring you into it at all,' he added hastily, knowing I was keeping the news of my parents' separation off the school's front page. 'His parents didn't talk for weeks either. Then one day – bingo – they're back together again.'

'Exactly how long were they separated for?' I asked.

'Tim said it was about eight weeks.'

So this meant I had just three weeks to go before my parents were back together. I even started marking the days off my calendar – sad but true.

I passed on Lee's words of wisdom to Claire too. I was amazed at how pally we'd become. Most nights we'd chew the fat for a while.

And then one evening she said this girl in her class called Tamzin was holding a party, and would I like to go with her. I was pretty shocked actually, that Claire wanted me, of all people, to accompany her. I assumed it would be one of those parties where the highlight is a game of musical bumps. So I politely, but firmly, declined the invitation.

And at the last minute, Claire didn't go either. Instead, after school she flopped into the kitchen and announced that she couldn't go to the party as she didn't feel very well.

Mum was immediately concerned. 'What's wrong, love?'

'I've got this bad headache and my throat is

sore and I feel shivery all over.' She said this remarkably calmly but Mum got worked up enough for both of them and immediately bundled Claire upstairs.

Later, I thought I'd better take a quick peek at the patient. I expected her to be fast asleep. And at first I thought she was. She was curled up in a ball with both hands wrapped around a woollen monkey, which she'd had since she was an amoeba and, incidentally, was called George. But then I heard the unmistakable sound of crying. And Claire wasn't just shedding a little tear, she was really sobbing her heart out.

I was shocked.

Then Claire sprang up, shoving the monkey away from her in an embarrassed way. 'What are you doing here?'

'I thought I'd just look in. Why are you crying?'

'I wasn't.'

'Oh, it must have been George then. Do you feel bad?'

'Terrible.'

'Do you want me to get Mum?'

'Don't you dare,' she cried so fiercely that I stepped back.

'OK, I won't get Mum. Do you want to talk to me?'

'I don't want to talk to anyone,' cried Claire.

'Just leave me alone!' She buried her head in the pillow.

I hovered. I couldn't just leave Claire sobbing away. Finally, I sat down on the green chair in the corner. It creaked.

'Are you still here?' Claire murmured.

'No, I left some time ago . . . This chair's really hard.'

'I never asked you to sit on it.'

'That's very true. Claire . . .'

'What?'

'Would you like to hear the funniest joke in the entire world?'

'No.'

'This guy walks into a fishmonger's with a mackerel under his arm. He says to the fishmonger, "Do you sell fish cakes?" The fishmonger says, "Sure, why?" And the guy replies, "Thank goodness for that, it's his birthday today."'

Claire was sitting up and looking at me now. 'That joke is pathetic.'

'Well, I've got a million like it. And I'll sit here and tell you every one of them if you don't tell me what's wrong.'

She hesitated.

'Joke number two. There's this man . . .'

'No, all right,' she said, lowering her voice and

generally acting as if she thought a microphone might be hidden somewhere. 'I've been telling everyone that Dad is away in America. But today I saw this group of girls from my class giggling and whispering and looking at me. Then they came over and Tamzin shouts, "Your dad's not in America at all. One of your neighbours told my mum what really happened. Your parents have split up. Go on, tell the truth!"

'And I kept on saying, "No, they haven't. Dad's just away on business." But Tamzin wouldn't have it. She got madder and madder until finally she was screaming at me, "Your mum and dad have split up and I bet it's because of you!"'

I was shocked. 'That is so nasty. Well, I hope she finds worms in her birthday cake. It's also total rubbish about Mum and Dad breaking up because of you. You're the golden girl.' And I couldn't stop a note of sarcasm escaping into my voice. 'The perfect child in every way.'

'No, I'm not!' declared Claire, indignantly.

'Oh, come on, you're the queen of the gold stars. How many did you get today? A thousand? And look at your bedroom, not a thing out of place.'

'I do bad things too.' Claire sat up. 'Like, I'm not really ill, you know.' She enjoyed my start of surprise. 'Fooled you, didn't I?'

'Yeah, you did actually.'

'I just couldn't bear going to Tamzin's party tonight. So I thought it'd be easier if I pretended to feel groggy. I'm going to have a little break from school and all my dear friends, who are probably gossiping about me at this very moment. In fact, I'm not planning to return to school until Monday at the earliest.'

'You're actually going to skive off school?' I exclaimed.

'Yes.'

I shot up and walked to the door. 'Excuse me a moment,' I said.

'Where are you going?'

'I think I'd better just go outside and check the world hasn't ended.'

'You don't know me as well as you think,' said Claire triumphantly. 'No-one does.'

I sat down again. 'On Monday, or whenever you go back to school, I'll go with you to see Tamzin. And I'll back up your story totally.'

'You'd do that?'

'Mighty kind of me, isn't it?'

Well, on Monday, Claire went back to school and at breaktime I confronted Tamzin. In a very dignified voice I said, 'But of course my father is in America, he's in Detroit, Michigan, on a special sales initiative.' Then I shook my head at her and said sternly, 'How could you listen to stupid gossip, especially about someone who is supposed to be your friend? I think you owe my sister a huge apology.'

And actually Tamzin did splutter out a 'Sorry, Claire', before going bright red and fleeing.

Claire was incredibly impressed and grateful. And I felt like a proper big brother. I even said, 'If ever you're in trouble, just come and see me, all right?'

Then later that day, by a freaky coincidence, Dad called to say he was going away for a while. Only it was to Belgium, not America. Still, it felt a tad strange, pretending something and then it sort of happening.

But much weirder than that was how Dad sounded. I mean, normally he'd be cracking a few jokes but today he was very subdued . . . and just different somehow. I told myself that it was because he didn't want to leave his two wonderful children, and who could blame him?

But, still, I had a horrible feeling that it wasn't just that.

Something was wrong.

Chapter Seven

That Sunday, instead of Dad we had a special guest appearance from Nan and Grandad, all the way from deepest Norfolk.

Nan and Grandad have been together so long their marriage is in the Domesday Book. Yet, they don't seem to have any interests in common. Grandad, since he's retired, spends all his time playing snooker and golf. While Nan prefers yoga, Keep Fit and thimbles. (That is not a joke, she really does collect thimbles and has got about four hundred of the boring things.)

And they're always squabbling and criticizing each other. Like today, Nan's first words were, 'Sorry we're late, but one of his snooker pals turned up and of course, we couldn't tell him we're on our way out. Oh no!'

'He had something important to tell me,' protested Grandad.

'Important!' Nan spat the word back at him. 'What could be more important than seeing your daughter and grandchildren?'

I wondered suddenly if Nan and Grandad had ever actually separated. They must have. So how did *they* get back together again?

I decided to try and get the low-down from Nan. My moment came when Mum, Claire and Grandad went out into the garden. Nan had to stay indoors because the sun gave her a headache. So I made her a cup of tea then said, 'Nan, can I ask you a very personal question?'

'You can ask,' replied Nan. You've probably guessed that she isn't one of those cuddly, fluffy nans who smell of lavender and think everything's wonderful. No, my nan is very outspoken and blunt, but she's funny and I like her a lot.

'Well, my question is . . . and if you get it right you win today's star prize.'

'Get on with it,' she snapped.

I took a deep breath. 'Did you and Grandad ever split up for a while?'

Nan's eyebrows shot right up. Then I think she figured out why I was asking her that and her expression softened – a little. 'No, your grandad and I have never separated. I've thought of it sometimes, though.'

'Have you?'

'I don't know a woman who hasn't. Not if she's honest. You see, marriage isn't all romance and rapture like people nowadays expect: it's work. Very hard work. And most of it will be done by the woman.'

'Really?'

'Oh yes. Look at your grandad. I doubt he even knows where the kitchen is. He couldn't boil an egg to save his life. He'd certainly never think of cooking me a meal for a change or even washing a cup. And I doubt he'd recognize a hoover if he fell over one.

'You see, in the old days, men went to work and that was thought to be enough. The wife did everything else. Things are different now, of course. Women won't put up with what they used to. They expect more from a husband. And if they find themselves in a rut they don't stick it out and hope things improve. No, they jump right out of that rut.'

'Is that what Mum has done?'

'Well . . .' Nan hesitated.

'Come on, Nan, tell me the truth. I am involved. And do you think Mum and Dad will get back together soon?'

'I hope they do,' said Nan. 'I really do but . . .'

'Yes?'

Nan put her teacup down with a bit of a bang.

60

'It doesn't help that your father lives in a dream world all the time.'

I bristled a bit at this. I didn't like to hear my dad being criticized by anyone.

I think Nan must have noticed because she said, 'I like the man and it can't have been easy for him never knowing his father, and losing his mother when he was . . .'

'Twelve,' I prompted. 'And he had a really nasty stepfather too, who sent him off to boarding school and . . .'

'Yes, I know all that,' interrupted Nan. 'But even so.' She spread out her hands. 'What's he doing with all those models and silly videos cluttering up the place? And the time he wastes on them.'

This from a woman who collects thimbles and has got line-dancing videos . . . But I didn't say anything. I was finding out things.

'Your father is so absorbed in his fantasy world, he doesn't see what's going on in front of him,' she continued. 'Your mother always puts a good face on things. She's like me there. But she's been unhappy for a while. I know that. But he missed all the signals, and in the end . . . well, your mother's been taken for granted once too often. That's how I see it anyhow.'

'They're not talking at all now, you know,' I murmured.

Nan shook her head. 'Your mother offered him a meal, tried to keep things civilized and he was very rude to her, in front of you and Claire too.'

'He was upset because Mum had painted the bedroom walls yellow without consulting him.'

Nan brushed this aside. 'If only your father would . . .' She hesitated.

'What, come on, tell me Nan, please?'

She gave a wintry smile at my enthusiasm. 'If your father could just come round and admit he should have done more, recognize that he's the one at fault here. Make the first gesture.'

The more I thought about that, the more I was certain Nan was right. It can't have been much fun for Mum doing all the work every night. Not once had Dad offered to do the cooking or hoovering or take her out for a meal.

Yes, that was it: I was sure if Dad offered to take Mum out for some nosh – and pay for it of course – that would ginger things up no end. I told Claire my idea and she was very keen.

Now I just had to sell it to Dad.

Well, he seemed to be away for ages. And when he finally did get back I suppose I was a bit over-eager. You see, two whole months had gone by.

So Mum and Dad should be reuniting now. And I know you couldn't really count the last two weeks as Dad had been out of the country. But still, I felt we were definitely playing in extra time now.

So maybe I pushed the plan too hard. Anyhow, it went down like a lead balloon. Dad showed absolutely no interest in making the first move and taking Mum out. I played it down to Claire but actually, it was quite a blow.

To make matters worse, the rest of my chat on the phone with Dad had been pretty uninspired too. I felt his mind was elsewhere. He seemed very, very remote. Was he worried about something?

The next time he called was no better. Dad seemed far away. Maybe he didn't like living on his own. Well, Claire and I didn't like him living on his own either. That's why I tried suggesting again – very tactfully this time – the meal out. But again, I got nowhere.

Claire picked up the same vibes as me. She said, 'Dad's not himself, is he?'

'I think he's homesick,' I replied.

He was supposed to be dropping round on Sunday as usual, but at the last minute he had to cancel because he'd got flu and didn't want us catching any germs.

'Couldn't you put a mask on?' I suggested. 'You could come as Darth Vader or ...'

Dad gave a throaty laugh and said, 'Sorry, but I'm stuck in the house at the moment.'

'Do you want Claire and me to come and see you?' I asked. 'We're both house-trained now and ...'

'I'd love you to visit,' interrupted Dad. 'But not right now.'

'So how are you managing in the house all on your own?' I asked.

'Oh, I'm getting along OK. Rachel looks in on me every day and generally keeps an eye on me.' Then he changed the subject and started going on about the new *Star Trek* model he'd bought recently and how it was a real collector's piece.

It was only afterwards that I thought again about Rachel. She partly owned Fantasy Adventure with my dad and a huge, red-faced guy called Dave. Rachel was very pretty. Actually, I had a crush on her once – for about a day. She was kind of dazzling, with what seemed like miles of dyed orange hair and all these amazing rings on her fingers and on her nose. She knew a lot about *Dr Who* too.

Well, it was nice of her to look in on my dad every day. Very nice. And I didn't think much more about her until I briefed Lee on the latest developments. As soon as I mentioned the fair Rachel, he gulped hard as if he'd just got hiccups.

'What is it?'

He made a face. 'I could be completely wrong.'

'Tell me.'

'Well, you haven't seen your dad for a while, have you, and when you have spoken he's been a bit vague, as if he's preoccupied with something else.'

'Yeah.'

'My dad was exactly the same when he started seeing his girlfriend.'

I let that bombshell just hang in the air for a moment.

'No way, mate.'

'OK.'

'For starters, Rachel's years younger than my dad.'

Lee just looked at me. I didn't need reminding that his dad was centuries older than his girl-friend too.

'But you're the one,' I said, 'who's always saying my mum and dad are going to get back together.'

'I'm sure they will,' said Lee. 'It's just, if your dad is seeing this girl and I know it's a big if – but if they are, that does change everything. I'm only trying to be honest with you, mate.'

'I know.'

'Look, tell me exactly what your dad said about Rachel.'

I wracked my brains. 'He just said she was looking in on him every day.'

'Every day,' echoed Lee ominously.

'And she was keeping an eye on him. That was all. He spent most of the time talking about this new *Star Trek* model he'd bought.'

'*Star Trek*!' cried Lee, a look of relief shooting across his face. 'You're all right, then.'

'Why?'

He lowered his voice confidingly, like a doctor about to tell you something very personal. 'Well, if a man gets into *Star Trek*, it usually means he hasn't been around a woman lately.'

'I never knew that.'

'Oh yeah, it's a known scientific fact.'

'Wow.'

'I read it somewhere . . . at least I think it was *Star Trek*. No, it definitely was.'

I was laughing with relief now.

'Hooray for *Star Trek*, is what I say.'

Chapter Eight

A few nights later, Mum was yarning on about how busy she'd been at work that day. And as she says that every evening I wasn't exactly listening. But then she added something new: very casually, she told us that a friend from the bank would be popping round tomorrow night to give her a hand with all the work.

Claire immediately asked, 'What's her name?'

'Roger Salmon,' replied Mum.

'That's a funny name for a woman,' I said.

'He's a very important person based in the big office a few miles away. I'm very lucky to get his help.'

Well, Claire and I weren't exactly on red alert. If a guy came round to help Mum with her homework, that needn't be a big deal. But we were suspicious though. Claire, especially.

She found out a few more things about him: he

was in his forties, wasn't married and was tipped to go right to the very top. In other words, a right little swot.

Well, the following evening this massive dark blue Jaguar pulled into Dad's space. I hated seeing that. I know it was the obvious place for him to park. But that was Dad's space and it should have remained empty until he came back.

We caught a glimpse of a man in a long coat (even though it was a warm April evening) getting out of the car. He was carrying a case. He looked a bit like a doctor making an early evening call.

Mum started babbling excitedly. 'This is so kind of you. I do hope you didn't have any trouble finding me.'

'No trouble at all, thanks to your excellent directions.' He spoke through his nose and had a kind of whiny voice. Then he gave this short cough. He sounded like a seal barking for a fish. Claire looked at me and gave a nervous giggle.

Mum said, 'Do come into the kitchen, I've prepared us a little snack . . .' and we couldn't hear any more. So we settled ourselves in the sitting room to watch *The Simpsons* marathon on telly.

A couple of hours must have gone by then we heard footsteps in the hall.

'He's leaving,' I murmured.

'About time,' replied Claire.

But then the sitting-room door opened and Mum was saying, 'Mr Salmon wanted to say hello,' and there he was.

What did he look like? Well, picture if you will, a six-foot gnome, with thinning black hair and serious teeth. He was wearing a very smart suit and was very clean-looking; even his fingernails gleamed. When he shook hands with me, I noticed that he smelt expensive too.

He plonked himself down in Dad's chair and looked so pleased and at ease, you'd have thought he'd been sitting there for years.

Claire was looking both scared and angry, as if the wicked witch of the west had just sat down opposite her. But I tried to be a bit cool about the whole thing. Even when he asked for the television to be switched off. I mean, I'd have turned it off anyway. And he did sort of apologize.

He said, 'I'm sorry, but I'm not a television watcher. I only watch golf and the weather, really.'

'The weather's my favourite programme too,' I said.

Claire gave a splutter of laughter. But then I thought, give the geek a chance, so I asked him what he actually did at the bank.

Now, I enjoy conversing with older people. I can chat with an old biddy at the bus stop and love it. But Roger was the most boring man in the entire universe. He just droned on and on about himself. It was like having the dullest lesson you can imagine brought to your house. In a minute I thought, I'm going to have to get some matches to keep my eyes open.

Suddenly Roger asked me, 'And do you get any pocket money?'

'Yes,' I replied, cautiously.

'And may I ask how much of it you invest?'

Mum laughed delightedly as he went on to tell me about all the different children's accounts and how much interest each one yielded. In a moment, I thought, he's going to ask me whether I've started a pension plan yet. And I knew he was just saying all this for Mum's benefit, because he kept looking across at her and smiling.

To be honest, he couldn't take his eyes off Mum. Actually, for her age, my mum is still incredibly unwrinkly. She's very tall and slim with red hair and she's got this dead cool air about her, especially when she's all dressed up for work.

I'd have been a bit worried about Roger's intentions if he hadn't been such a complete saddo.

After he'd gone, Claire was exclaiming, 'Oh, wasn't he awful? He just talked about himself the entire time.'

'Don't bother about Roger,' I said. 'We'll never have to suffer him again.'

I was so wrong.

Two things happened over the next few days: first of all Mum got promotion. She was dead chuffed and we were pleased for her. She said that although she was taking on more responsibilities, most of the extra work could be done at home. So that was all right.

Then Mum told us who she was working on a special promotion with . . . ah, you've guessed, haven't you?

And yes, very soon Roger was back round our house. He called earlier this time, not long after Claire and I had got back from school in fact.

We went upstairs to do our homework. But I couldn't really concentrate. And much more surprising, Claire couldn't either.

So then we decided to listen to some CDs in my room. But before the first track had finished Mum was calling up the stairs asking me to switch the music right down.

'I bet that's because of Roger,' I said. 'Loud music probably makes his ears bleed or something.'

Later, Claire and I trooped downstairs to the sitting room to see what was on the telly. We'd hardly sat down when a rather flustered-looking mum popped her head round the door. 'I've asked Roger to stay and have something to eat with us. Will you look after our guest, children, while I get everything ready?'

We couldn't exactly say no, could we? So off went the telly again and then Roger started firing questions at us: what was our favourite lesson? when were our next exams? what sports did we like? I was sure he'd got those questions out of a book.

Then he started telling us about his school days. 'Now when I was at school, well, get your head around this . . .' And he was off with some totally pointless yarn. On and on he went until Mum called, 'Children, will one of you set the table, please?'

I was about to spring up – anything to get out of here – when Claire mouthed at me, 'Oh let me go, please, please.'

Should I be kind and let Claire escape instead of me? I was pondering this weighty matter when Roger piped up, 'Your mother has just asked one of you to set the table.'

Claire and I were completely shocked. What was he doing sticking his nose in? It was absolutely nothing to do with him.

And then – would you believe – he went on to say, 'If your mother's good enough to cook you a meal, I think the least you can do is go along and help her. Don't you?'

That was so out of order, Claire and I could only gape at him. How dare he start lecturing us? He had no authority here. For a few seconds my throat was so full of swallowed anger, I couldn't speak.

Finally, I recovered enough to say, 'Claire, you can go and help Mum,' swivelling right away from Roger while I said this.

'Thanks Joe, I will,' she replied.

After Claire had left, Roger only started cross-examining me again. 'Now, tell me, what are your hobbies?'

I considered. 'My top hobby is looking under my bed. I can do that for hours. It's just brilliant fun.'

Even Roger caught the mocking sarcasm in my voice and didn't ask any more questions. Instead, we just sat there in silence (which suited me fine) until Mum called us to the table.

Claire and I weren't rude or cheeky during the meal but we weren't exactly bursting with life either. In fact, we both adopted this forlorn, drab manner talking in low voices and looking thoroughly miserable. I was kind of enjoying myself. Yet I was angry too.

Why was this man suddenly being inflicted on Claire and me? He was nothing to do with us, yet he seemed to think he could order us about.

Roger left straight after the meal. He didn't even stay to have coffee. What a shame!

There was a furious gleam in Mum's eyes now. 'What on earth was the matter with the pair of you, acting like two orphans of the storm all through tea. I didn't know where to look.'

'We don't like him, Mum,' whispered Claire.

'Oh, really?' exclaimed Mum. 'And do you suppose I like all your friends? Yet, I'm always polite and friendly to them, aren't I? You don't deserve the present he left for you both.'

'Present?' Claire and I exclaimed together.

'Yes, he gave you ten pounds each. I said there was no need but he insisted.'

'We don't want anything from him!' said Claire.

'All right,' cried Mum, thoroughly exasperated with us. 'The money is on the table in the hall. If you don't take it I shall be very pleased to spend it myself.'

We took the money intending to post it right back to Roger in the morning. Only we didn't. Then Claire suggested burying the money in the garden. But I thought that was a bit daft. So finally, we didn't do anything with the tainted money at all. It just hung about like a bad smell.

And I kept wondering why Roger had given us this money. We hadn't exactly been chummy with him. Was this his way of keeping us quiet while he went on seeing our mum until finally he married her – and then immediately packed us both off to boarding school . . .

I was thinking wildly now. But I didn't like, or trust, Roger. And I hated seeing him in my house, and his car parked in Dad's space.

And where was Dad anyway?

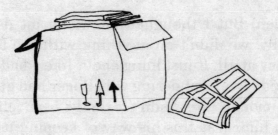

Chapter Nine

At last Dad called to say he'd be round on Sunday. Claire and I eagerly awaited his return to the old homestead. But – guess what – on Saturday night he rang to cancel again. It seemed his flu was still kicking around and he wouldn't be able to make it after all.

I felt cheated and let-down. Surely he could have popped in for half an hour. I didn't say much to Claire: no sense in getting her stressed out. But I did bend Lee's ear about it.

Then on Sunday afternoon the phone rang and it was Lee. I was pretty surprised because I knew his nan and grandad (from his dad's side) were paying their annual visit and they usually whisked him off somewhere.

'I'm on a payphone, so I can't talk long.' His voice sounded odd.

'Where are you?'

'In the town centre,' he replied. 'They're buying me a few things.'

'Excellent. Keep them at it.'

'But I . . . I,' Lee spluttered and then went quiet. After which the pips began to go.

He shoved some more money in and I asked, 'What's wrong, mate?'

'Probably nothing at all.' Then he gulped right in my ear. 'Only, I've just been into Fantasy Adventure and your dad's in there with that girl Rachel . . . I just thought you ought to know.'

I felt as if I'd just swallowed something very heavy, but I managed to say, 'Yeah, you did the right thing. Thanks for telling me, mate.'

Then the pips went again and Lee had to go. I put the phone down. I was stunned and very angry.

What was happening to my parents?

First of all Mum inflicts Roger on us, who, after five minutes in our house, thinks he can start telling Claire and me what to do. And now there's Dad, who'd rather mess about in a shop with a girl young enough to be his daughter than come and visit his own children.

Dad probably never had flu at all. That was just a way of fobbing us off so that he could spend more time with her.

I pictured Dad in the shop grinning and

flirting with Rachel, while she flicked her hair about and laughed at everything he said. I could see it all as clearly as if I'd been peeping through the window at them.

And it wasn't good enough. Dad had responsibilities. He couldn't just abandon Claire and me. But dads do that. Lee's dad for a start. Lee never even saw his dad for nearly a year.

I looked at my watch. The shop stayed open until five o'clock on Sundays. So I had just over two hours to get the bus into town and see my dad and say . . . well I wasn't quite sure what. Maybe I'd just stand there for a moment and let him see that I knew all about him and Rachel and how he wasn't really ill, and then just disappear again.

I thought it was best no-one else knew about my mission (Mum might try and stop me anyhow). So I told Claire and Mum that I was going round Lee's house.

Then I sped off to the bus stop and had to wait so long that it was nearly four o'clock by the time I got into town. And Fantasy Adventure is not exactly in the centre of things. In fact, it's tucked away down a really narrow, dingy side street. But there's nothing dingy about the shop. Its window is always crammed with eye-catching posters and displays.

The doorbell plays the opening bars of the *Star Trek* theme which make you feel at home right-away. (Dad wanted our doorbell to play the *Star Trek* theme tune too, but Mum absolutely refused.)

And once you're inside, you just don't know where to look: there are toys, games, videos, CDs, books, comics all crammed into quite a small space. Plus there are huge cardboard cut-outs of Buffy (from *Buffy the Vampire Slayer*) and Batman (Adam West from the TV series). And there's a secondhand section too called 'Collectables'.

Normally I feel a little glow of pride, gazing around such an epic shop. But today was different. Today, looking around it just gave me a horrible sick feeling. There was no sign of my dad but Rachel was there, serving the only customer in the shop – a man in a battered-looking leather jacket. He placed his purchases in an equally battered-looking bag, put a pair of giant headphones on and left.

Rachel cooed with pleasure when she spotted me. 'Oh Joe, this is a surprise. I haven't seen you for ages. You've got taller,' she added, as if she was telling me something I wouldn't have noticed.

She looked so happy to see me I was quite

taken aback. There wasn't even a flicker of embarrassment.

'So how are you?' she asked confidingly. She was wearing even more rings on her fingers than I remembered.

'I'm OK,' I said, a bit curtly. 'I've come to see my dad.'

She actually said, 'Oh, good.' Then she went on, 'This bug has knocked him really hard. And now Dave's caught it too. That's why your dad stepped into the breach . . .' Then she added, as the shop was now completely empty, 'We were so busy earlier. Anyway, your dad's in the stockroom sorting out our mail orders which have been piling up.' She laughed. 'Oh, your dad will be so pleased to see you. I'll take you down to him rightaway.'

Once, years ago I'd been allowed behind the counter and down into that most secret of places, the stockroom, and I'd been so excited. I'd sat on the safe, gazing around in wonderment at all those unpacked boxes (they let me unpack a few) and discontinued toys and posters. The dead and the unborn mingled freely here. And presiding over it all was a cardboard cut-out of Captain Kirk.

Well, everything was just as I'd remembered it, except for my dad.

I did a double-take of shock when I first saw him. It wasn't just that he looked so pale and ill, but he was so scruffy too. His hair was all greasy and lank, the shirt he was wearing had stains all over it and he just looked totally sad and un-cared for and suddenly, so much older. It was as if four years had passed since I'd last seen him, not four weeks.

He was parcelling up some orders when he spotted me. At once he sprang to his feet.

'Is everything all right?' he asked, his large brown eyes – spaniel's eyes, Mum had once called them – fixed on me.

'Everything's fine.'

'Claire's all right?' persisted Dad.

'She's flying.'

'And your mother?' he asked in a much lower tone.

'Flying too.'

A look of relief spread over his face.

'Joe's just popped in to see you, Nick,' said Rachel, 'which is really lovely.' Then the *Star Trek* theme tune rang out and she had to dash upstairs.

'Well, well,' said Dad. 'So you've just dropped in.'

'Yeah, I thought I'd remind myself what you looked like.' I was certain now that Dad hadn't just dumped Claire and me, as I'd feared. And I was pretty doubtful about him and Rachel being a couple too. They certainly didn't act like one. And to be honest, Dad looked such a complete mess, it was hard to imagine any woman with reasonable eyesight fancying him at the moment. But I still felt a pinch of anger that Dad was here in the shop and not at home with Claire and me.

I said, 'I'm surprised you haven't come by to see us.'

Dad smiled apologetically. 'I thought if you see me like this I'll scare you both out of a year's growth.'

'We've missed you,' I said.

Dad looked pleased and a bit surprised. Then he set about making me a cup of coffee. He went into overdrive, looking for and never finding the biscuit tin, and then he discovered there wasn't any milk either.

'I was sure there was some still left.' He shook his head in utter amazement. 'Well, there'll be some upstairs.'

A few minutes later he came down again waving a jar of powdered milk. And I noticed how out of breath Dad was: a quick sprint up and down the stairs and he was puffed out. All Dad's energy seemed to have just leaked away.

'I'm afraid this powdered milk is pretty vile,' he said.

'The more disgusting it is, the better I'll like it.'

'You're going to love this coffee then,' laughed Dad. 'And I'm afraid the spoons have walked too. So you'll have to stir it with a pen.'

He plonked the mug down. 'John Steed from *The Avengers* always stirs his coffee anti-clockwise, says it helps the flavour.'

'And this coffee needs all the help it can get,' I joked.

Dad suddenly put back his head and laughed. And then he seemed to relax a bit and chatted with me about the new stock which was coming in. But all the time I was thinking, it's not just because of the flu he'd let himself go. Living on his own was making him really miserable. He was totally lost and missing Claire and me – and yes, Mum too.

And then the *Star Trek* bell began to do its stuff over and over.

'We always get a rush just before closing time,' said Dad. 'So I suppose I'd better give Rachel a hand.'

'Yeah. I've got to be back for tea anyhow.'

'You can't be late for that,' replied Dad. But he said this quite good-humouredly.

Upstairs, Dad insisted on ringing a taxi for me.

And while I was waiting he told me to pick anything I wanted – and see if I could find something for Claire too.

And then Dad was swooped on by this old guy who was looking for a 1969 *Doctor Who* annual which he hadn't been able to find anywhere else. Dad rummaged about in the Collectables section and then brought out the very annual. All that man's chins started wobbling with excitement. And over and over he said, 'I can't believe it. I've been searching for this annual for so long.'

Dad told me once his greatest joy was hunting down stuff for people. And I could see why he liked that bit best.

I left him in his little kingdom, still chatting with that customer. I bet he dreaded stepping out of there and going back to an empty, lonely house.

When I got home Mum was painting the sitting room. 'I'm sorry, Joe,' she said. 'Tea's going to be a bit late tonight. I thought I'd be finished long ago – but I've been held up.'

Then Claire hissed at me, 'Joe, quick, I've got something really important to tell you.'

Chapter Ten

We went up to Claire's room, and she was skipping about so excitedly I said, 'If you don't calm down I'll go and get one of those tranquillizer guns they use on elephants.'

'I can't help it. You'll never guess who just called round.'

'Amaze me.'

'Roger.'

'What!' But then I saw how happy she was, so I asked, 'What happened then?'

'Mum took him into the sitting room. And I thought I'd better creep down to hear what they were saying.'

'Good for you,' I interrupted, thinking how Claire would never have done such a thing a few weeks ago.

'He was just talking away in his usual, dull way at first,' continued Claire, 'but then he said

85

to Mum, "I've brought you a little present, some chocolates which I hope you will like . . . sweets for the sweet."'

'He never said that?'

Claire nodded.

'Sometimes there's just not enough vomit in the world, is there?'

'And you should see the chocolates he's brought Mum! A massive box with three layers and all tied up with a blue ribbon.'

'He's throwing his money around now, but just wait until he's got Mum. Then I bet he'll be as tight as two coats of paint. By the way, I hope this story improves soon.'

'Oh it does, but just let me tell it,' cried Claire.

'Go on then.'

'Then he asks Mum if she'd like to go out for a meal.'

'In other words, a date. He's got a nerve,' I muttered.

'He suggests one day and Mum says no. Then another and she says, "No, that's not convenient either". And finally, Mum says, "Roger, would you mind if we leave it for now? I really value you as a friend so much, but you see, I am only separated from my husband."'

'Mum said that?' I cried.

'Every word. I felt like cheering.'

'I bet you did. What did Roger say after that?'

'Not much. In fact he left almost straight away. I only just got back upstairs in time.'

'That is fantastic news,' I said.

'And it shows what I've been saying. Mum really is missing Dad.'

'And Dad is missing Mum too,' I said.

'How do you know?'

'I've just seen him.'

I couldn't help enjoying Claire's look of total astonishment. Then I told her all – or practically all. I left out my suspicions about Dad and Rachel (I was totally certain there was nothing in it now).

By the time I'd finished, Claire's lower lip was starting to tremble. 'Oh poor Dad,' she cried.

I nodded.

Then she added somewhat accusingly, 'Your friend promised Mum and Dad would come to their senses in eight weeks . . . but now twelve weeks have gone by and they're still not even speaking to each other.'

'Well you can't blame Lee for that.'

'I'm not.'

'It's just our mum and dad have lost the plot, big time.' I looked at Claire. 'I think it's up to us to do something.'

'What exactly?'

'I'm not sure.'

Claire considered. 'We could go to Mum and tell her what a state Dad's in. She's bound to take pity on him.'

'She might – but I don't think it's such a good idea.'

'Why?'

'Well, when Mum and Dad broke up we know it was Mum who chucked Dad out, don't we?'

'Yes.'

'And I wouldn't be massively surprised if one day Mum just decided she was sick of looking after Dad all the time and wanted a break from him. So if we go to her now and say Dad's in trouble and needs looking after, she'll just think, "Here we go again, me doing all the work as usual," and be even more annoyed and fed up with him.'

'I see what you mean,' agreed Claire. 'I just don't like leaving Dad on his own.'

'Neither do I.'

Then Claire gave a little squeak. 'I've got another idea.'

'Let's hear it then.'

'Why don't you move in with Dad for a while? Then you can look after him . . .'

'And check he eats his greens,' I interrupted. 'Hey, that's brilliant!'

'Thanks.'

'So brilliant I can't believe you thought of it,' I went on. 'Maybe I could improve Dad a bit too: sort out his appearance for a start. And teach him to be more useful about the house. And how to cook a few meals. Up to now, all Dad's cooked in his life is toast. Well, that's going to have to change.'

'Then in a few weeks' time we'll unveil the new improved Dad,' cried Claire. 'And Mum will be so impressed . . .'

'She'll take him back on the spot,' I interrupted. 'It's a dazzling scheme!'

'The only thing is,' said Claire, 'well, I did think of the idea first.'

'You did.'

'And yet I'm not doing anything.'

'Oh yes, you are. You're a crucial player in all this. You've got to ensure this remains a Roger-Free Zone for the next few weeks. I'm certain he'll try and stage a comeback.'

'Are you?' A look of fear came into Claire's eyes.

'Well, look at those chocolates he bought Mum – I bet they were the most expensive ones in the whole shop. And he's been throwing his money around at us too. Remember those ten-pound notes he gave us?'

Claire sighed.

'But don't you see, Roger's forking all that cash out for a reason, to impress Mum. And he's not going to let one little setback put him off. No, he's probably sitting in his house right now, plotting his next move to win Mum over. So you've got to be on guard all the time.'

'I will be,' replied Claire, keenly.

'And try and work on Mum psychologically.'

'How do you mean?'

'Well, get her remembering the good times she had with Dad. We want her thinking nice thoughts about him again. So, you can see your role is absolutely vital.'

Claire was very happy now. 'And when do you think Dad Mark Two will be ready?'

'I reckon I'll need about six or seven weeks to really spruce Dad up. So that brings us to about the middle of July. Then we'll try and pick a special occasion . . .'

'Like your birthday on the 18th,' interrupted Claire.

'Perfect!' I exclaimed. 'Mum and Dad will have to be in the same room that day, so it's a top chance for Mum to see how massively Dad has improved and then – well, happy endings all round.' I added, 'But we mustn't let them suspect what we're doing. If they do, the whole operation could be blown.'

'And we mustn't tell anyone else either,' said Claire.

We looked at each other. This felt like a very significant moment.

'We ought to have a code word for the operation,' cried Claire eagerly. 'How about DM2 – short for Dad Mark Two?'

'DM2 it is,' I agreed.

Then we heard Mum calling us downstairs.

Claire looked at me. 'I suppose Mum will let you go and stay with Dad.'

Now I hadn't thought about that.

Chapter Eleven

'Mum, can I talk to you for a minute.' That was me, on Monday evening.

'You can talk to me for two minutes if you like, dear.' That was Mum all bright and breezy. She'd just finished painting the sitting room for the second time, having decided that turquoise – the colour she'd painted it yesterday – was too cold and draining. So now she'd painted it white. She seemed well chuffed with her handiwork so I figured this would be a good moment. I'd already alerted Claire, who was hovering upstairs.

'Now Mum,' I began, 'I don't want you to take this the wrong way, all right?'

Mum had this little smile on her face, thinking I was about to say something funny.

'And this is absolutely nothing against you, all right. But I'd like to check out Dad's lodgings and stay with him for a while.' However casually

I tried to say the words they still landed with a giant thud.

And at once all the colour just drained from my mum's face. This was going to be so horrible.

'But why do you want to do that?' she asked in this funny, muffled voice.

I'd figured she might ask me that and began reciting an answer I'd prepared earlier. 'Well, Claire and me, we're here together, while Dad's just in his house all by himself. And I don't think he should be on his own, not all the time. So I'd like to keep him company.' In my best Dracula voice, I added, 'But have no fear. When the wind changes I will return.'

Then, as Mum was just sitting there looking completely stunned, I burbled on, 'It will give you a welcome break from me and my annoying little habits. Just think how great it will be to pick up a cushion and not find one of my socks underneath it. You're going to have a great time without Public Nuisance Number One under your feet all the time, aren't you?'

Mum turned and looked right at me. I could almost hear her brain whirring away. Finally, she said, 'I'm going to tell you something that will shock you.' Normally I'd have said something silly in reply to that. But Mum was looking so serious that for once, I didn't.

93

'I see a lot of myself in you,' she said.

Now I had to laugh. 'You're joking.'

'No.'

'But you can't have been as bad as me at school.'

'Oh, I think I was,' replied Mum. 'I certainly had your laid-back attitude to things like exams and homework. And my parents thought it was up to me if I worked or not, and so I didn't. Then of course I failed just about every exam I sat. And I saw all my friends moving on while I was held back for another year.'

This was fascinating stuff, but why was Mum cracking open her album of memories right now?

'It took me a long while to catch up – well, you remember me going to all those evening classes.'

'I sure do.'

'And Joe, I don't want you to make the same mistakes as me. That's why I'm always telling you to get on with your homework. Last week for instance, when you had that geography coursework to do and I kept saying, "Don't forget it's due in tomorrow." I know I'm nagging you and it's very annoying. But I want the best for you.' She paused. 'I realize your father is much more relaxed about these kind of things.'

Now I knew where Mum was coming from.

'That has got nothing to do with me leaving, Mum.'

'And you probably would have more freedom with your father . . .'

'Mum,' I repeated. 'That has got nothing to do with me leaving.'

This time she heard me. 'So why?'

'I've told you why. I just want to spend a bit of time with Dad. That's all. Honestly.'

'And how long do you plan to be away?'

'Six or seven weeks at the most, no longer.' Suddenly this whole conversation seemed a bit freaky: here I was telling my mum how long I'd be away, just as if I were the parent, not her.

'So you'll be home again . . . ?' asked Mum.

'On my birthday, July 18th. That's a promise.'

'And you've spoken to your father about this?'

'Yes, I have.'

Actually I'd just chatted very briefly with him on the phone. I'd said, 'Dad, this is your lucky day. If Mum agrees, I'm coming to stay with you on Sunday night for a while.' He sounded extremely surprised but said that I was welcome anytime. And that was it. I'd swapped homes in less time than it takes to boil an egg.

'And when are you planning to leave?' asked Mum.

'Sunday teatime, if that's all right with you?'

'You will come back and visit, though?'

'Of course I will . . .' Then I added as gently as I could, 'Mum, I'd really like to do this.'

'Would you? I see.' Mum just sat there for a moment, looking sad and defeated. 'Well, if you've set your heart on it, I can't really say no, can I?'

'Thanks, Mum. You're a star.'

Shortly afterwards, the phone rang. Mum answered it while Claire was hissing at me from the doorway, 'So what happened? Did she say yes?'

'She did, although she's a bit choked about it all. She thinks I've changed sides.'

'Oh no!' said Claire. 'Still, it's for her own good really.'

'You're right, it is.'

'And I've started on operation DM2 already. Do you want to see?'

I followed Claire up to her bedroom. On her wall now was a collection of family snaps, most of them taken on holiday. Now, my mum is a big fan of the rustic side of things. Show her some trees and a gang of cows and she's happy. So our holidays were always spent deep in the country-side in one of those cottages which seem to just bob up miles from anywhere.

Mum thought the cottages 'very pretty and

charming', but they were also about the size of a doll's house. So Dad would walk in and instantly smack his head on the beams and then pretend to pass out.

All the cottages, but especially the rickety old stairs, were hazardous for someone of Dad's size. He'd joke, 'Every time I go upstairs I take my life into my hands.'

And Dad was always breaking things too. Once Dad sat down on a stool which promptly fell apart. He tried to put it back together, but couldn't. And in the end I took a picture of him holding up the broken stool with a daft grin on his face, while behind him, Mum was trying very hard not to laugh.

That picture was up on Claire's wall, as was the one I'd snapped a few moments later of Mum holding up the stool. Only she couldn't pretend to be serious about it any more and was just laughing away.

To tell the truth, I think those country holidays were a big endurance test for Dad (he'd have much preferred to be lying on a beach somewhere). But he never once got sour or grumpy. Instead, he just larked about and generally acted as if he was having the time of his life.

'Now Mum can see how things used to be,' said Claire, 'and how much fun she and Dad had.' Her voice began to wobble. 'When I get married I won't let anything change. I'll just make sure everyone stays happy for good. I really will.'

'And who do you think is going to marry you?' I teased.

Mum appeared in the doorway. 'Has Joe told you his news?' she asked Claire. 'He's leaving us for a while.'

'Yes, he told me.'

'We're going to miss him, aren't we?' continued Mum.

'We might,' smiled Claire.

Over the next few days, Mum put on a brave face about my leaving. She didn't give me a hard time at all and on Sunday afternoon even helped me pack.

We took the cases downstairs, after which Mum handed me a note. 'This is for your father,' she said. 'Just a few little suggestions and . . . well, make sure he gets it, won't you?'

'I will.'

'I've also put some things in a box for you. There's a casserole and some cakes. And in case your father hasn't had time to stock up yet, I've put in a packet of your morning cereal and a few other things. I think I might even have slipped in a packet of your father's favourite biscuits.'

Just after five o'clock we set off – Claire too –

to find Dad's house. None of us had even seen it before. It was on a busy road right on the outskirts of town, with shops, a leisure centre and three pubs. There were a few houses right at the top. Dad's was the last one of these.

Mum and Claire helped me out with the bags.

'We won't come in,' said Mum.

Claire looked as if she was about to protest, but then she saw Mum's tense face and changed her mind.

Mum gave me a big hug and told me not to forget to come and see them soon.

As they were leaving, Mum called out of the window, 'Well, have a lovely time, you two.' Then she drove away really fast and I walked up the path to my new home.

Chapter Twelve

I buzzed on the doorbell, and moments later there was my dad popping out of a house which I'd never even seen before. I can't tell you how weird that was. Perhaps that's why I felt a bit awkward and shy.

Dad smiled nervously. He wasn't sure what to say either. So in the end he said, 'Here you are.'

To which I replied, 'Yeah, here I am,' and then felt oddly out of breath. Changing homes really takes it out of you, you know.

Dad stretched out his hand and we shook hands just as if we were meeting for the first time. It was all so peculiar. The whole thing.

'Did your mother bring you?' asked Dad.

'Yeah, her and Claire.' Then I added, 'They've gone now,' just in case he thought they were hiding somewhere.

'Ah, yes,' said Dad. 'Right.'

'So how are you feeling, Dad?'

'Oh, much better thanks,' replied Dad firmly. He didn't look much better. He was unshaven with great bags under his eyes and an alarming collection of angry red spots on his face. He had also, I noticed, put on a great deal of weight and now looked as if he had a small rugby ball tucked under his shirt.

'Well, Joe, welcome to my humble abode. I should just warn you, there's not enough room to swing a cat in here.'

'It's all right. I've given up swinging cats for the moment.'

Dad gave one of his big hearty laughs. 'We're going to have fun, aren't we? Well, let's get your bags in. Hey, are all these yours?'

'They certainly are.' And I suddenly realized my dad hadn't a clue how long I planned to stay with him.

'And what's in the box?' he asked.

'There's some food and stuff from Mum. Oh yeah, she's put in a packet of your favourite biscuits too.'

I think Dad was a tiny bit choked when I told him that, because he looked away from me and muttered, 'That was kind of her.'

We lugged the bags into the hall which, with Dad and me in it as well, was now looking distinctly crowded.

'We'll leave the bags there for now,' said Dad, picking up the box. 'And I'll show you the kitchen, which I've just tidied up in your honour.'

Dad had certainly cleared the kitchen table of rubbish and the sink was fairly clean too. But the bin under the sink was just brimming over with rubbish. And that is one of Mum's pet hates. She'll say, 'Doesn't anyone else notice when the bin is full? Why is it always left to me?' In a certain mood she can talk for ages on this subject. I made a note in my head: must train Dad to empty bins regularly. And on the floor by the bin was a large, dirty tea stain. Something else Mum hates ('All you've got to do is squeeze the tea bags in the sink before throwing them away'). So Dad was going to have to put in some work on the way he handled tea bags as well.

'Well,' he said, looking round at the kitchen and then at me. 'We're going to make this a half-term to remember, aren't we?'

'Actually, Dad,' I said, gently, 'half-term finished two weeks ago.'

'Did it?' Dad looked astounded.

'Yes, and I'm planning to stay a bit longer than

the next few days. Mum's written you a note about it.' I fished it out of my pocket.

Dad took the letter and started pacing around the kitchen. 'Ah right. Yes,' he murmured. Then he said to me, 'So is everything all right at home?'

Talk about a daft question. Of course everything wasn't all right at home. He wasn't there for a start. Had he forgotten that little fact already? But I just said, 'Oh yeah, Claire and Mum are rocking.'

'And let me get this straight. You'll be going from here to school tomorrow and for the next seven weeks?'

'That's right. Mum's given me a letter for school explaining my temporary change of address, and actually – if it's not a total pain – could you give me a lift there before you go to work?'

'I'm not back at work yet.'

Now it was my turn to be astonished. Dad seemed to have been away from his job for yonks.

'And at the moment, I'm without a car too. It's being repaired, I'm afraid. There is quite a good bus service, though.'

My heart sunk a bit at having to mess about with buses. Up to now I'd been able to walk to school in about ten minutes. (I still managed to be late most days but that's another story.)

Later, Dad found a bus timetable. Actually, I had to get two buses – and my journey began each morning at four minutes past seven which is a prehistoric time to even be awake, never mind moving things like legs and arms.

'Sorry about that, Joe,' continued Dad.

'Oh, not to worry,' I said, pluckily. 'You'll have your car back soon.'

'I hope so,' murmured Dad, a little too vaguely for my liking.

'Anyway, let me give you a tour.' This didn't take long as there was only one other room downstairs: the sitting room. It was smallish, cosyish with a cream-coloured sofa that, to be honest, had seen better days and seemed to groan for mercy every time you sat on it.

But there was a truly massive television, a video and a state of the art CD player in there as well. Also, decorating the room were generous numbers of papers, magazines, foil trays, video boxes and crinkly chocolate wrappers, while lurking in the corner under the window was a plate, which, judging by the interesting-looking mould growing on it, had been living there for quite a while.

Mum would not have been amused.

Then we took the bags upstairs to my room. Now, I'd been expecting something pretty small and I wasn't disappointed. But I had thought there'd be at least a proper bed in it.

Yet, as Dad explained, Roy (the owner of the house who'd gone abroad for a year) had lived alone and used my room as an office. So Dad had moved the desk from here into his bedroom and brought in a fold-up bed made, at a guess, just before World War I.

Dad found me a duvet, then apologized that there wasn't a wardrobe (or indeed anywhere to hang my clothes except for two hooks on the door). But he said I could use his wardrobe next door.

Then he pulled down the blind on the window which immediately shot up again ('a bit temperamental') and switched on the dimmest light bulb I'd ever seen (no lampshade, of course) and asked: 'What would you like to do?'

'Leave now,' was the reply which immediately sprung to mind. But I just shrugged my shoulders while Dad said, 'I'll leave you to get unpacked and settle in, while I go and ring for some food.'

I hung about in my room for a while, but I didn't unpack. I just sat on the floor feeling totally homesick, to tell the truth.

But then I decided I was behaving like a silly little kid. After all, I was a man on a mission. What did shallow things such as a proper bed and a wardrobe matter? I had much more important concerns. And I started jotting down in my diary.

OPERATION DM2 (DAD MARK TWO)

Day One:
Dad's appearance: Awful. Needs to shave, go to bed early, lose weight and get better clothes.
Dad's bad habits: Too many to list them all. Urgent training needed here.

Then I wandered downstairs, and Dad couldn't have heard me, because he was sitting in the kitchen with such a blank look on his face it scared me. It was as if Dad wasn't there any more and had somehow vanished inside his own head.

'Dad,' I cried. He gave a little jump and smiled at me.

'Hey, where were you?' I asked.

'Just thinking, that's all.'

Moments later, the doorbell rang and our food arrived. Dad and I scoffed the pizza in the sitting room and had the chocolate biscuits – which Mum had sent – for afters.

On the wall was a massive photo of *Alien* depicting the moment when the evil creature starts bursting out through a man's stomach. It's

106

a great scene, though not perhaps the ideal thing to stare at when you're eating.

'So, Roy's pretty keen on sci-fi films too?' I said.

'Oh yes,' replied Dad. 'Roy's one of Fantasy Adventure's most regular customers. Which reminds me . . .' A gleam came into his eye. 'They've just released on video for the first time, the original pilot episode of *Dr Who*.'

This is a really big deal if you're a fan of *Dr Who*. And I would say it's impossible to live with Dad and not be infected by his enthusiasm. Except of course, Mum and Claire have managed to do just that.

Mum has certainly never watched an episode of *Dr Who* all the way through, let alone *Star Trek*, *The Prisoner* or *The X-Files*.

But anyhow, I was excited about seeing the pilot episode of *Dr Who*. So as soon as we'd finished eating ('We can clear away later,' said Dad) we watched this antique, black and white episode on Roy's wide-screen telly.

And it was great, except I only managed to see the first half hour. You see, Dad doesn't just watch a video. He pauses, and rewinds, and studies a scene again and again in slow motion. And he's always got so much to tell you. Like that night he freeze-framed an expression on an actor's face. 'Look closely, Joe, that is really good acting.'

Dad hadn't missed a thing in that episode. I wondered how many times he must have watched it already. It was as if he loved it so much he couldn't let go. At one point he said to me, 'You must be really sick of seeing this in slow motion.'

But actually, it was great, because Dad was just like his old self again: really happy and relaxed and making silly jokes. And for a while everything felt normal again.

Then I went upstairs to bed and lay there in the dark listening to the wind whistling. I thought I'd never get off to sleep but I did.

I woke up about half an hour later though. And for a moment I didn't know where I was. But it quickly came surging back.

And then I heard an unexpected noise coming from the landing. Someone was moving about out there.

'Dad?' I hissed. No answer.

I heard a creak on the stairs.

'Dad?' I cried again.

Still no answer.

It couldn't be a burglar, could it?

I took a deep breath and scrambled out of bed.

Chapter Thirteen

I stood at the top of the stairs watching this figure sneaking towards the door. He was acting as if he were a burglar making off with his booty (or whatever burglars call it these days), when actually he was . . .

'Dad!' I yelled.

This time he heard me all right. He swung round, stared up at me and said, 'Joe! Did I wake you?'

'Unless this is all a dream, yes, you did.'

'I was trying very hard to be quiet. Sorry.'

'But what are you actually doing?' I asked.

'I'm just slipping out for a while.'

'But it's . . .' I squinted at my watch. 'It's nearly half past eleven.'

'Yes, I won't be long.'

'Where exactly are you going?'

Dad hesitated. He wasn't about to tell me he

was meeting Rachel somewhere, was he? But instead, he said. 'Look, it's best I show you. Put on your dressing-gown and slippers and come downstairs.'

I don't actually wear slippers. And I haven't done since I was about two months old (even then I knew they were totally uncool). But I decided in the stress of the moment Dad must have forgotten that vital fact, so I bunged on my dressing gown and trainers. Then, bursting with curiosity I scrambled downstairs.

'Follow me,' said Dad.

'Where are we going?'

'Only to the garage.'

We went through the little gate at the end of the back garden and down this pathway. There was a moon floating about in the sky like a giant bubble and turning Dad's hair silver. No-one else seemed to be about.

We reached the block of garages. Dad's was bang in the middle. He fumbled about for his keys then said to me, 'You're going to laugh now.'

'Am I?'

'Oh yes, you're going to be very amused by your old dad.'

He yanked up the garage door. I don't know what I was expecting to see, but certainly not a silver and blue motorbike.

I'm not massively keen on motorbikes (I prefer cars) but I recognized it as a Harley Davidson: one of those *Easy Rider* bikes with lots of chrome and big handlebars which are pretty old-fashioned now.

Dad was watching my reaction to the bike really closely. In fact, he was practically breathing down my neck. 'So, what do you think?'

'Well, yes . . . . it's a good bike.'

'You're thinking, what's your ancient old dad doing with one of those?'

'No, I'm not. And you're not ancient.'

'It's an investment really,' said Dad, hopefully.

'Right.'

'And motorbikes are quite cheap to run,' he went on. 'Cars cost a lot more money. And I've always wanted a bike like this.'

'I didn't know that.'

'Yes,' he nodded. 'Of course, there was no chance of my stepdad helping me to buy one. And then when I passed my test and was finally able to afford a bike, well, I got engaged and cars were the thing. So that was that. But I saw this one recently and thought I've got to have it . . . and it will certainly go up in value. So it's money in the bank really.' Then he picked up his crash helmet and put it on. 'Anyway, I'll be back soon.'

'You're going out on it now?' I exclaimed.

'Yes, of course.'

'Bit late, isn't it?'

'No, this is when I usually go out on it. The roads are clear, so no-one gets frightened by the sight of me on a motorbike.'

'When will you be back?' I demanded.

'By midnight.'

'No later,' I said.

He grinned. 'No later, I promise.'

'Well, OK,' I said doubtfully, but I just didn't like the idea of my dad speeding off on a motorbike so late. Especially as he'd only recently started riding one. And people have accidents on motorbikes all the time, don't they – particularly at night.

'Just take it easy now, Dad. And if you put a dent in that motorbike it's coming out of your pocket money.'

He chuckled, then revved up the engine. A look of what I can only call sheer delight crossed his face. 'I always loved that sound . . . Joe, go straight back into the house now and pull the door tight, OK?'

'OK.'

Dad waited until I was inside, then drove away. At first, I couldn't help thinking this was all a bit freaky. But then I considered it some more and decided, actually, it wasn't freaky at all.

After all, when I'm feeling stressed out, the first thing I do is take off on my bike for a while. And it really does help to clear my head. So the motorbike is just helping Dad to clear his head. And there's nothing wrong with that, is there?

I went back upstairs and tried to get to sleep, but I couldn't. I wanted to hear Dad safely home first. So in the end I wandered back down into the kitchen again. Then I decided I'd have a pot of tea waiting for him when he got back. He might want some munchies too. So I put out some more of the biscuits Mum had sent him onto a plate.

He returned, as he'd promised, just after midnight.

'Enjoy yourself, did you?' I asked.

'Yes, yes,' said Dad rather bashfully. 'And you should be in bed.'

'I thought you'd like a cup of tea.'

Dad saw the tray of tea and biscuits and then smiled at me. 'Bit of a midnight feast, this.'

We sat chatting and chewing for ages. Then, just as I was going upstairs, Dad said, 'There's no need to tell your mother about the motorbike. I don't think she would approve.'

I was certain she wouldn't.

Still, I thought it was a good sign that Dad cared what Mum thought of him.

'Don't worry, Dad. Your secret is safe with me.'

But I decided I would tell just one other person – Claire.

Chapter Fourteen

I saw Claire on Saturday. But there was no time to talk, as Mum took us to the science museum and was kind of ever-present the whole time.

Then on Sunday, Claire came round to Dad's pad. We didn't go out anywhere (his car was still being repaired) but it was just good to chill out together.

Later, Dad popped out to the launderette with a pile of stuff, including my PE kit. As soon as he was out of earshot, Claire began to get really upset.

'Oh, Joe, I can't believe it. He looks awful.'

'I know.'

'And so much older: he's even getting an old man's stomach. What's happening to him?' she exclaimed.

'He's been on his own too much, that's all. Now don't start going all droopy on me.'

'I'm not!' cried Claire, indignantly.

'He needs a lot of work, but we're on his case now. I've already made masses of notes about him in my diary.' I looked in my pocket. The diary wasn't there. 'I must have left it upstairs.'

'You're getting as absent-minded as Dad.'

'Oh, cheers.'

'Before you get your diary, I've something to tell you: Roger rang up on Friday.'

'What did he want?'

'He wanted to speak to my mother,' said Claire, doing quite a nifty impression of Roger's voice. 'But luckily Mum wasn't in and I forgot to give her the message.'

'Nice one.'

'But the strange thing is, Roger started chatting to me and being all pally.'

'Yuk!'

'He said he was sorry if we'd got off on the wrong foot but he didn't have any children of his own, and he hoped we'd give him another chance.'

'Talk about creepy.'

'I know. He just went on and on, too.'

'What did you say?'

'Well, not much. I was so shocked. In the end I pretended there was someone at the door.'

'He thinks if he gets in with us, Mum will like

him more. That's why he gave us that money.'

'I still haven't spent mine,' said Claire.

'Neither have I,' I replied. 'I can't, somehow.'

'Maybe we should just burn his money,' continued Claire.

'Yeah, maybe,' I began. 'But the important thing is to stop him getting back with Mum and . . . anyway, let me get my diary. I've made some important notes.'

I shot upstairs to my bedroom but I couldn't find it. Then Claire called out, 'I've found it. It was on the little telephone table. And you've got a message on the answerphone. Shall I play it?'

'Yeah, go on, because I bet it's Lee. He was supposed to call me yesterday.'

I sprinted down the stairs again. I'd just reached the bottom step when the answerphone started up.

And the caller wasn't Lee.

Instead, a voice said, 'Nick, it's Jimmy Craig here. I've just heard the news and I can't believe it. Everyone in the office is really shocked too. We all think the company is insane letting you go. So look, give me a bell when you can and . . . keep your chin up. You're already being missed.'

Then another voice – a woman's voice this time – announced, 'That was your last message.' And the answerphone clicked off. I was still standing on the bottom step, my heart thumping fit to burst.

Claire slowly turned round and began to walk towards me. 'It's a wrong number, isn't it? We're always getting them on Mum's answerphone from people we've never heard of. Just the other day . . .'

'No, it's not a wrong number,' I said slowly.

'But it doesn't make any sense!' cried Claire.

Yet, in a way it did. I'd wondered how Dad had managed to be absent from work for so long, and I'd thought it was odd that his car was taking all this time to repair. I'd half suspected something was wrong. Now I knew.

'So, has Dad ben sacked then?' asked Claire, her face ashen.

'I think he has. Yeah.'

Claire sank down onto the bottom step of the stairs. I crouched beside her.

'Poor Dad,' she croaked. 'He's lost his family, his home, and now his job.'

'Not to mention his car,' I murmured.

'Oh, I hate all this happening to him. I hate it, I hate it!' Claire's green eyes flashed angrily, but tears were sneaking down her face too. I gave her hand a quick squeeze. She looked at me. 'Dad's good, isn't he? Even that man on the answerphone said that.'

'He's the best salesman they'll ever have,' I agreed. 'But since he's broken up with Mum – well, he has let himself go a little, hasn't he . . . ?'

'But they should be helping him,' interrupted Claire. 'After all, he's worked there for years.'

'More than twenty years,' I said.

'How can they just chuck him out like that?'

I shrugged. 'I don't know.'

Claire wiped her eyes with her sleeve, then asked, 'Do you think we should tell Dad that we know?'

'No, I don't,' I replied firmly.

'Why?'

'Well, when I get a bad report the last thing I want is people seeing it and feeling sorry for me. It's private. And so is losing your job. Dad will tell us if and when he wants to.'

Claire considered for a moment, then said softly, 'I think you're right.'

'And anyway,' I went on, 'Dad will get another job – probably a better one than he had before. And meanwhile he'll still get some money from Fantasy Adventure and when they sack you, they give you some cash too, don't they?'

'Redundancy,' whispered Claire.

'That's the baby. Well, Dad will have that, although he's blown most of that on a motorbike.'

'What!' exclaimed Claire.

'Yeah, it's stuck in the garage. Dad's been going out on it at night.'

'Oh no.'

'Don't worry, I've been discouraging him from doing that. He found me a helmet and has taken me out on it a couple of times. But most days, he just polishes and cleans the bike now. Don't tell Mum, by the way.'

'Of course not.' Claire squeezed her eyes shut. 'What a total mess. Everything's going wrong, isn't it?'

'No, it's not. But at the moment, Dad's only got us. That's why we've got to be there for him. And we've got to be strong.'

'I know.' Claire let out a soft intake of breath. 'But what about Roger?'

'What about him?'

'Well, what chance has Dad got against him with his big flash car and big flash job and . . .'

'Every chance,' I practically shouted, 'because Roger is just a boring little cockroach and Dad, well he's . . . great really. And Mum must have thought so once, or she'd never have married him. Unfortunately, he's now also developed some annoying little habits. I've been noting them all down. But I'm going to iron them out starting tomorrow when I begin Phase Two of the master plan. Here, take a butcher's at what I'm going to do.'

This is what she saw:

1) **D's Cooking**

D has never cooked a meal in his life, always leaves it to M. Even if he comes home the same time as M, waits for her to get the food ready. The reason is simple: D cannot cook. I am going to change this by teaching him some basic meals.

2) **D's messiness**

D never cleans up after himself, leaves it all to M. She finds this annoying. I am going to train D to clean, dust, use a hoover, etc.

3) **D's appearance**

He is looking old and ill and has bad skin. He needs to go to bed earlier, get new clothes and new haircut. Most importantly, he must lose weight. At the moment the only exercise D gets is when he's laughing. This must change. Regular exercise and better food (see 1) essential.

'But this is brilliant,' cried Claire.

'What's brilliant?' asked Dad. He seemed to just pop up out of nowhere.

Claire slammed my diary shut. 'Er, what's brilliant,' she began 'is . . .'

Seeing she was floundering, I cut in. 'This new band.'

'Oh, what are they called?' asked Dad.

'DM2,' I replied, quick as a flash.

'Catchy name,' said Dad.

I flashed a grin at Claire. 'And they're a band who make things happen.'

Just before Claire left, I hissed, 'Don't forget, be on your guard against Roger at all times.'

'Don't worry, I will, Joe.'

'And look out for a new improved Dad, starting tomorrow.'

Chapter Fifteen

The following evening Dad was sitting in the kitchen going through the Yellow Pages. 'Now, we've had Indian, Chinese and pizza, so how about tonight . . .'

'Cooking some good nourishing food ourselves?' I interrupted.

I don't think Dad could have looked more astonished if I'd suggested going out and picking wild berries for tea.

'Ah, well you see the trouble is, I'm not exactly a master chef. Your mother was the expert at all that sort of thing.'

'But I thought we could just do something really simple, like scrambled eggs on toast. I've got some eggs and some bread.' I pointed at a bag on the side.

'So you have,' cried Dad. 'Where have they come from?'

'From the local shop up the road. The woman in there is really nice. And she told me they've had people in there buying eggs and bread before. Isn't that amazing?'

'All right,' laughed Dad. 'We'll try scrambled eggs. But I bet tomorrow you'll be begging for pizza again.'

I thought, no I won't. But I didn't argue, just said, 'The eggs are there and the bowl and the whisk, so go ahead, Dad, make my eggs.'

Dad picked up the eggs and walked slowly over to the bowl. He cracked them with surprising ease.

'Hey, superbly done.'

'It's all in the wrist,' he said. 'Never had a cookery lesson in my life, you know.'

I was shocked. 'But we have a double period of it every week!'

'I'm afraid we were only ever allowed to do woodwork or metalwork. So I had a fine collection of eggcups and keyrings.'

'Very useful.'

'And I made a tea-tray. And a candle holder.' He chuckled. 'Once I even tried to make a chess set. But that was a bit ambitious. You see . . .'

'You must tell me all about that one day,' I interrupted hastily. 'but right now could you pour some milk into the bowl and start whisking?'

'In other words, stop yakking,' smiled Dad. 'Right, here we go.' He poured in a generous portion of milk, then proceeded to whisk those eggs with everything he'd got. Yolk was soon flying out of the bowl. Some even made it onto the curtains.

'Hey, Dad, you're not doing DIY. There's no need to beat those eggs to death.'

Ten minutes later, Dad and I sat down to scrambled eggs on toast, covered in tomato sauce, with maltesers and ice-cream for afters. And it all tasted delicious. We both smacked our lips appreciatively.

'I really enjoyed that,' laughed Dad, 'despite my over-enthusiastic whisking. Still, I think I've got the hang of it now.'

'Oh, you'll be whisking with the best of them soon. Now, I've also bought some bacon. I thought we could have bacon and eggs tomorrow.'

'But I must pay you for all the food you've bought. I insist on that.'

Dad waved a ten-pound note at me. When I told him the entire cost of our meal was only £2.80 he was stunned. 'Is that all?'

'If you cook for yourself, it's a lot cheaper than takeaways, isn't it?' I said.

'It certainly is!'

Then I decided to press on with the next part of my campaign. This was going to take a little tact, however.

So I began by saying, 'Dad, if you like, I'll help you to clean the house up after tea.'

Dad started in surprise.

'Actually, what I've done, is draw up a little rota.'

'A rota,' echoed Dad.

'And here it is,' I said, bringing it out of my pocket. I'd done the rota out properly too, with our names at the top and the days of the week at the side.

I started to read from it. 'Now, what I'm suggesting is that on Monday, you clean the sitting room while I do the bathroom. Then on Tuesday, you do the kitchen while I sort out the bedrooms. On Wednesday, there's the hall, stairs and landing to do. So I don't know if you've got any special preference.'

Dad didn't answer me. He was just staring at me, open-mouthed.

'Well, how about if I do the stairs and hall, and you do the landing? We can always swop later. Then on Thursday we can just check out what we've done in the week. I expect the kitchen and sitting room will be the main rooms to clean again and on Friday we've got a night off. How does that grab you?'

Dad was looking a tiny bit affronted now. 'So you think the house needs cleaning then?'

'Well, it could do with a bit of a spruce-up, couldn't it?'

Dad shrugged. 'I can't say I've noticed.'

'Here, let me show you then.' I took him into the sitting room, then I pointed down by the radiator. 'Take a look there.'

Dad looked. 'I don't see anything.'

'I think you'll need to get down on your knees to get a proper look.'

So Dad got down on his hands and knees and then began peering under the radiator.

'Do you see anything now?' I asked.

Dead silence for a moment. Then Dad exclaimed in a voice full of wonderment. 'Yes, I do.' He picked up a giant piece of fluff and turned it over in his hand. 'There's loads of this stuff down there.'

'I know.'

'It's just strange that I never noticed it before.'

'Well, you're tall. So you're above the dirt line really, aren't you?'

'Yes, I suppose.' Dad went on to crawl around the rest of the room. It wasn't long before he'd hunted down more dust. 'It's everywhere. This room is filthy. I can't believe it.'

'You just needed someone to point it out,' I said.

He got to his feet. 'Now, I wonder if there's a hoover anywhere about.'

'Yes, there is. I found it in the cupboard under the stairs.' I wheeled it in. Dad hoovered as forcefully as he whisked eggs, determined to track down every bit of dust he could find. Neither of us could locate anything that looked remotely like a duster though. So in the end I suggested he use a pair of his old socks, and they did the job just fine.

The following day when I got home I was assaulted by an alien smell. That stale savoury, meaty fragrance which had haunted the house (and my clothes) ever since I'd arrived had been knocked out by the aroma of polish. For a moment I felt quite giddy with shock. Dad was waiting for me in the kitchen, grinning like a madman.

'Look around you,' he said.

I did. And I was truly, truly amazed. Only one word could adequately describe our kitchen now: spotless. I bent down. 'You've even got rid of all the stains around the bin.'

'It's taken me all afternoon – and I never

realized housework was so tiring – but I got there, didn't I?'

'You certainly did.'

'I've also gone and kitted myself out.' He pointed at the dusters, brushes, cans of polish and dustpan on the table. 'Now, go and take a look upstairs.'

Well, he'd only gone and tidied up there too, in a most spectacular fashion as well.

'Dad, I can't believe how neat and clean everything is. But I was supposed to do the bedrooms tonight.'

'No, it's not right you having to clean up in the evenings. If I need any help with your rota, I'll let you know. But I'd rather you got on with your homework . . . Ah, I've just said a horrible word, haven't I?'

'You certainly have.'

Dad patted me on the back. 'You've a right to a clean house, so if ever anything looks messy or dirty just tell me, all right. Now, we're cooking again tonight, aren't we?'

'Yes, we are.' And seeing he was in such good spirits I thought this might be a good time to press on with the next part of my plan.

'Dad, the school's been telling us how we've got to try and get fit.'

'Very good,' said Dad.

'And they've suggested we go out for a run every night.' (This was a total lie but it was in a good cause.) 'They also said, in the interests of safety one of our parents might want to accompany us.'

'Ah,' said Dad swallowing hard.

'But don't think about that yet,' I went on. 'Enjoy your bacon and eggs first.'

Chapter Sixteen

The following evening I strolled into my local shop which was empty apart from the lady behind the counter. 'Hi, how are you doing?' I asked. We always have a little chat.

'I'm very well. But I want to know how you got on with the bacon and eggs.'

'In the end, it was great.'

'In the end,' she repeated.

'Yeah, well Dad's what you would call a highly enthusiastic cook. He must have chucked half a bottle of oil into the pan yesterday.'

'Oh dear.' She began to chuckle.

'And he overcooks everything. The bacon was all shrivelled up. I mean, it shuddered when it saw me.'

She began to laugh.

'And we had smoke everywhere. So we had to open all the windows. But then we had another bash and this time the bacon was only a little bit burnt and we soon got used to the smell of smoke. So it was brilliant, really. Anyway, I'm after something for tonight now.'

She popped out from behind the counter. She was smallish and very quick in her movements, darting about all over the shop. I would say she was quite an attractive woman of about forty-five (but I'm hopeless at guessing ages) with amazing hair: it was a smart grey colour, if you know what I mean, and very bouncy. She also wore three large rings on one finger, one of which was a wedding ring.

'How about some nice ham with new potatoes?' she suggested.

'I hadn't thought of new potatoes.'

'Well, they're very tasty at the moment and you haven't got to peel them: just wash and boil them. And you must start having some greens as well.'

'Really?'

'Oh yes, very good for the skin.'

'Well, OK,' I murmured, thinking of all Dad's zits.

'Now, I'd recommend the broccoli. I'll just give you one bunch. You won't need any more, as it doesn't keep very well. And how about a couple of bananas for afters?'

'Yeah, whack 'em in.'

She piled it all up on the counter. 'There you are dear, that should make a lovely meal.'

'Can I just ask you something? If your husband prepared that for you one night, would you be pleased?'

'I'd be very surprised. He's been dead for seven years.'

'Oh look, I'm really sorry,' I said, at once.

'Don't be. How were you to know? I still wear his wedding ring and always will. And yes, I would have been delighted had he given me that meal one night. He did used to cook sometimes, mainly at the weekends.'

Just as I was leaving, she said, 'Maybe you could do a prawn salad tomorrow.'

'Great idea. Thanks.'

'Well, I'm in here every night, after five o'clock. I'm Denise Hammond, by the way.'

I was chuffed that she told me her first name. Adults hardly ever do that, do they. That was very friendly of her.

'And I'm Joe,' I said. 'See you tomorrow then, Denise.'

'I'll be here.'

After that Denise helped me every evening. She even lent me this cookery book which had masses of good, simple ideas in it. She and I would chat for a bit too. She said I was the spitting image of her son, Paul. She even showed me a picture of him when he was about my age. And actually, there was a pretty uncanny resemblance (except, of course I'm much better looking. Ha Ha).

I'm like him 'in ways too'. So Denise reckons anyway. Paul's working in Germany now – he's been there for the past three years. You can tell Denise really misses him. But she's keeping busy: besides her job in the shop in the evenings, she works at the Leisure Centre during the day and at Help the Aged at the weekends.

One day Dad came into the shop and I introduced him to Denise. She immediately noticed how interested Dad was in the food now. And it was true. There was a little sparkle in his eyes when he asked me what we were cooking tonight. He also, to my great surprise, was sticking to the cleaning rota. And we'd started going out running too.

To tell you the truth, I nearly gave up on the running. The first time, Dad and I decided we'd run to the park, which was supposed to be two miles away. But that can't have been right as we were running for hours, sweat streaming down our faces. We kept noticing these two birds hovering overhead. They seemed to be following us.

'Are they crows?' I asked Dad.

'No, vultures,' he quipped.

When we finally reached the park, we just collapsed on the grass, gasping. Neither of us could breathe, let alone speak, for several minutes.

Finally, I managed to splutter, 'Look, it's tiring now, but we're going to feel like a million dollars tomorrow.'

Next day my legs hurt, my knees hurt and I had these horrible blisters on my feet. Dad was in an even worse state as he hobbled down the stairs (holding tightly onto the bannisters all the way), muttering, 'Every muscle in my body feels like it's been hit by a giant hammer.'

I'd have chucked in the running if Dad hadn't happened to be wearing a luminous, green shirt which vividly displayed his paunch. But that gruesome sight spurred me onto a second night's running with Dad. And a third . . .

After a while, to liven things up Dad and I started having these races home. At first, just to encourage him I let Dad win. Then I discovered he was winning anyway. So we really started racing after that.

Now, I still reckon running rots your brain. But I have to admit, the improvement in Dad was just incredible. Not only did he start losing weight but his skin problems began clearing up and he was even standing better. Before, he was always slouching about. But now he was standing with his shoulders right back.

It was all starting to get very exciting.

There was still the problem of Dad's clothes. Dad showed no interest in buying anything new. So Claire and I hatched a cunning plan. I told Dad I needed some new clothes. So he dutifully accompanied me into town. Claire popped up too. Then I pretended I couldn't find anything suitable. But Claire and I kept finding clothes that would 'look brilliant on Dad'. Claire was especially skillful at persuading Dad to try things on.

In the end he bought three new shirts (including a really smart denim one, which I wouldn't mind borrowing), two decent pairs of trousers and some new shoes too.

'He'll go down a storm in those new clothes,' I said. 'Mum will hardly recognize him.'

'And I can't believe how much slimmer he looks,' declared Claire.

'Do you reckon he's lost about a stone?'

'Oh, easily,' cried Claire. 'His paunch has practically disappeared. And he's walking much more confidently, isn't he?'

'I was hoping you'd notice that.'

'And what about his spots?' said Claire. 'They're all clearing up too. It's amazing. There's still his hair though.'

'I know. It just looks like a bird's nest at the moment. We must do something about that.'

'And how's he getting on with the cooking?'

'He's coming on. He still bungs everything on maximum and boils the vegetables until they fall apart. But he's got very keen. The other day I even caught him studying that recipe book Denise Hammond gave me.'

'Now that's a really good sign,' cried Claire. 'And guess what? Yesterday I found Mum in my bedroom looking at all the holiday pictures I'd stuck up. And she was standing right up close to them, as if she wanted to look at them properly. She was smiling too. Dad used to really cheer her up, didn't he?'

'He certainly did.'

'Well, I think she was remembering that.'

'Just wait until Mum discovers that Dad cooks and cleans now; she's going to be so happy.'

Everything was going just perfectly.

Until, right out of the blue, came Claire's SOS.

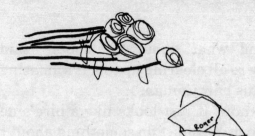

Chapter Seventeen

I'd just got home and was reading a note from Dad saying he'd gone to the launderette and wouldn't be long, when Claire rang.

'Thank goodness you're back!' she gasped.

'What's happened?'

'A couple of minutes ago the doorbell rang and there was this man delivering a massive bouquet of flowers for Mum. They were red roses, all wrapped up in silver foil wrapping . . .'

'Never mind that. Who were they from? Or let me guess: Roger.'

'Do you know what he wrote on the card? "May I take you out for dinner. Warmly, Roger."'

When a man asks a lady out for dinner, that's like the overture to asking her out, isn't it? I remember Lee saying that since Marti had taken his mum out for a meal they'd become as thick as

138

thieves. And Marti is round the house practically all the time now.

Could I imagine Roger round my house all the time? Only in my worst-ever nightmare.

'So has Mum seen the flowers yet?'

'No, that's why I rang you. She's at this important meeting. Shall I just throw the flowers away?'

'Yes,' I replied promptly. Then I thought a bit more. 'No, don't do that because he'll only ring up and ask Mum if she liked his flowers. And then Mum will guess what you've done and she might even take Roger's side.'

'I could pull some of the roses' heads off?'

'Nice idea, but again, Mum would only get mad at you and we want her mad at Roger,' I frowned, 'or disgusted by him. Or . . .'

All in a flash it came to me. 'Claire, listen. I want you to take the flowers and put them in your bedroom.'

'Right.'

'I'm going to try and get round to the house before Mum.'

'But how will you do that?' asked Claire. 'It'll take forever on the bus.'

'I won't get the bus. I'll use the ten pounds Roger gave me for a taxi. I can't think of a better use for his money, can you?'

Claire began to laugh.

'And I shall be bringing something with me.'

'What?'

'You'll see. But I'm going to sabotage Roger, good and proper.'

Less than half an hour later, I got out of a taxi. I made it stop a couple of roads away from my house. I didn't want one of the neighbours saying to Mum, 'I saw Joe getting out of a taxi today. I hope everything's all right.' It was vital Mum didn't know I'd been here today.

I paid the fare (£10.50 – daylight robbery) and walked briskly up my road. It was a very hot day but I was wearing a jacket, and concealed beneath that jacket was something vital for this mission.

Claire was waiting at the door for me. 'Oh great. You made it.'

'I said I would . . . and cheer up, won't you.'

She was so agitated, her face was all flushed. 'But what are we going to do? What's the plan?' she wailed.

I reached inside my jacket and then produced the ugliest, tackiest, most hideous plastic roses you've ever seen. 'Just feast your peepers on these. Aren't they mind-blowingly awful?'

140

'They certainly are,' cried Claire. 'Wherever did you get them from?'

'From Pat's flower shop. They were in the window half-price.'

'I'm not surprised.' A little smile flashed across her face. 'We're going to substitute these for the real roses, aren't we?'

'We certainly are. Then when Roger rings up – as he will – to ask Mum if she received his flowers, she'll say, "Oh yes, I did and they're lovely," because adults never tell the truth about things like that. But in her heart, Mum will be saying, "You're a man who sends plastic flowers to me. I'd never want to eat a meal with someone so gross and tasteless."'

'It's an idea of pure genius!' cried Claire.

'I thought you'd like it,' I said, giving a little bow. 'But come on, we haven't got much time.' I put the plastic flowers on the kitchen table. 'They're so ghastly I almost like them,' I murmured. 'Have you got Roger's card?'

'Yes,' said Claire. 'I was just wondering whether I should try and smudge the writing.'

'No, leave that. Those plastic specimens there say it all.' I placed the card beside the flowers. 'Perfect.'

Claire stared at my handiwork. Then she gave a little shiver.

'What is it?' I asked.

'Nothing, it's just . . .' She shook her head. 'No, it isn't anything.'

I smiled at her. 'I bet you've never done anything as bad as this before, have you?'

She flushed. 'Yes, I have.'

'What?'

'Well, I skived off school that time.'

'What else?'

Claire's flush deepened. 'Oh, I can't remember now.'

I grinned. 'Well, if anything goes wrong, just blame me.'

'I certainly won't. Don't forget I rang you. If I hadn't done that . . .' All at once, she tensed. 'I think I hear a car.'

She sprinted off, then dashed back. 'Yes, Mum's just pulled up.'

'Right, well she mustn't see me. Otherwise she'll get very suspicious, so I'll exit by the kitchen door.' Then I remembered something. 'But what about the real flowers? Where are they?'

'I put them in my bedroom, just like you said. And I had an idea about them. Why don't I hide them tonight and then tomorrow forge a card in Dad's writing and pretend they've come from him, and then . . . ?'

'No, no,' I interrupted. 'Dad's not even talking to Mum. Why would he suddenly send her flowers? And what if Mum rang him up to thank him. He wouldn't have a clue what she was talking about.'

Then, seeing Claire's crestfallen face, I added, 'It's an ace idea but too risky. I think it's best those roses are right off the premises. So I'll take them with me. Can you quickly get them now?'

She was up the stairs in two bounds and down them again in two more bounds. She handed me the flowers, her hands shaking slightly.

'I'll dispose of these,' I said.

I was about to go when Claire hissed, 'Wait, take this.' She thrust a ten-pound note at me. 'It's the money Roger gave me – for your taxi back.'

'Oh, well done. I'm practically skint as well, so you've saved me a long walk home.'

Then we heard a key in the lock.

'Give me a chance to get away,' I whispered. 'Keep Mum nattering in the hall for as long as you can. And talk loudly, that kitchen door is a bit creaky.'

Claire dived away. As I was edging towards the door I heard her say, 'Oh hi, Mum. I've been so worried.' She was practically shouting.

'But didn't you get my message, love?'

'Yes,' screeched Claire. 'But I still hated coming back to an empty house.'

'Oh love, I'm sorry,' cried Mum.

I was easing the door open now. It performed its usual wheezing noises but Claire was still shrieking about how much she'd missed Mum. She was giving a great performance.

At last I was outside. I carefully closed the kitchen door and I was just creeping past the window when I heard Mum and Claire come into the kitchen. Claire was saying, 'Some flowers arrived for you, Mum,' and I thought, I've got to hear this next bit.

'Some flowers for me?' exclaimed Mum, and you couldn't miss that little tremor in her voice. 'Oh, but what a lovely . . .'

And then she saw the flowers and made what I can only describe as a strange, gurgling noise, the kind a sink makes when it needs unblocking.

She did finally manage to murmur, 'Well, how very thoughtful of him.'

At this point I had to put a hand over my mouth to stop myself from laughing out loud.

'Who are they from?' asked Claire casually.

'They're from Roger,' muttered Mum. 'Very unusual, aren't they?'

'Shall I put them in a vase for you, Mum?' asked Claire (nice touch).

'Well...' Mum hesitated. 'Perhaps later. I must admit, I don't really like plastic flowers. They seem so unnatural – and unnecessary – somehow. I mean, there are so many beautiful flowers out there. Who wants artificial ones?'

Roger, I thought, you are well and truly snookered, mate.

But I didn't dare hang about any longer, as the last thing I wanted was for Mum to discover me skulking outside with a massive bunch of roses in my hand. So I nipped out of the back gate and then half-ran down the road, the flowers making a huge bulge under my jacket.

I made for the shopping arcade and quickly located the payphone. I rang for a taxi. And while I was waiting, I took a closer look at Roger's gift to Mum.

Now, flowers are definitely not one of my specialities but even I could tell these must have cost a bomb. Roger really was determined to weasel his way into Mum's life (and ours too). To be honest, he was making me feel more and more uneasy. I was glad it was only two and a half weeks to my birthday and the unveiling of our new, improved Dad.

I wanted to get rid of the roses, but I wasn't sure what to do with them. There were quite a few people around, and if I just threw them on to the ground someone was bound to chase after me with them. I was still deciding what to do when my taxi pulled up.

I bundled into the back with my flowers.

'Nice roses,' said the driver.

'Mmm,' I murmured.

'Are you courting, then?' He winked at me.

'Oh, no,' I said, quickly. 'I'm . . . I'm just looking after them for someone.'

'Taking the roses for a walk, were you?' Then he laughed at his own joke.

I got out a little way from my house. I certainly couldn't take these flowers home. Then I spotted a large bin. Perfect. I'll just hurl them in there. I was about to do exactly that when I heard a voice say, 'Hello, Joe.'

I looked up to see Denise Hammond smiling at me. 'How are you, dear?'

'Just fine, thanks.'

'Those roses are absolutely beautiful.'

And in that instant I knew exactly what to do with them. 'They're for you, actually,' I said, thrusting them at her. She almost fell over with shock.

'For me,' she faltered.

'Yes, I was just coming to find you. They're a thank-you for all the help and advice you've given me with the shopping, and for letting us borrow that recipe book.'

'But Joe, I haven't done anything, really, and these are so expensive. You can't afford this.'

'Well, Dad chipped in a bit too. Only,' I added hastily, 'he didn't want me to tell you. He's very shy like that. So if you see him don't even mention them to him.'

She was quite overcome. 'I don't know what to say. Do you know, I can't remember the last time anyone gave me flowers.'

'Can't you?'

'No, and how did you know red roses were my favourite?'

'Lucky guess. Anyway, I've got to go, so . . . enjoy. Bye!'

I rushed off, feeling quite pleased with myself. I'd saved Mum from Roger and made Denise Hammond happy. Not bad for an afternoon's work.

Chapter Eighteen

Then, twelve days before my birthday, Dad dropped a bombshell.

It was Sunday afternoon and Claire was round at Dad's house too. We'd just finished his chicken salad and the conversation had moved on to Dad's hair. Claire was in charge of getting him to have his hair cut and styled. And she was doing pretty well at persuading him, or so I thought.

But suddenly Dad sat back in his chair with an odd little smile on his face. 'I know exactly what you two are up to,' he announced.

Claire and I exchanged shocked glances. I felt myself go very still inside.

'Do you?' I said, as casually as I could.

'Oh yes,' replied Dad. That funny little smile had vanished now. He leant forward. 'The

148

message on the answerphone from Jimmy Craig. You've both listened to it, haven't you?'

'It was a total accident,' I said. 'I thought it was going to be from Lee. But yes, we've heard it.'

'And you know I've lost my job.'

'We kind of worked it out, yeah,' I replied.

'And we're really sorry,' chipped in Claire. 'It must have been a horrible shock.'

'Yes, it was,' said Dad. 'I'd been there twenty-two years . . . a long time.'

I thought that was all he was going to say. But then he started up again, in a voice as quiet as whispering.

'I've never been what you'd call ambitious. I just found a job I liked and stuck at it. I didn't want to go any further and end up trapped in an office all day. And my old boss and I got on like a house on fire.

'But last year, he took early retirement and this new guy moved in. A bit of a whizz-kid, or thought he was. Very young too, years younger than me. And from the start we didn't hit it off. Suddenly he was bombarding us all with these memos and extra paperwork. I just threw most of them in the bin.'

'Best place for them,' I interrupted.

'He sent us all these e-mails as well. I ignored

them too. I thought I'd been there so long it gave me certain privileges, like going my own way. But actually, it didn't. And when they started reorganizing the areas and decided they only needed four reps, instead of the five they'd had before . . . well, I was the one handed the short straw.'

'That's so unfair!' cried Claire.

'Still, it's their loss,' I said.

'No, it's my loss,' retorted Dad. 'I could have kept that job if I hadn't been so big-headed and stupid. I was very angry with myself. And I couldn't face you two at all. I felt I'd really let you down. That's why I pretended I was in Belgium.'

'When actually you were here all the time,' I said, gently.

'That's right. Then I got ill – I really did have flu – and just closed the door on everything, and then . . .' Dad paused. Claire and I hardly dared breathe. Dad was confiding in us and we didn't want to break the spell.

He went on talking more quickly. 'Then I just sat in here having a big think about my life – and getting more and more depressed. Soon I was no use to anyone.'

He looked across at Claire. 'Until your brother appeared, that is. He made me get on with things like cleaning the house: even had the cheek to give me a rota. And he's had me out running every night too.' He started to laugh now. 'He was determined I wouldn't have a moment to sit and feel sorry for myself. But I expect you're in on this too.'

'Yes,' smiled Claire. 'I am.'

'I thought so. A right pair of little schemers, aren't you.' He laughed again, and then banged the table so hard he made the cups rattle. 'Now I know you've had me doing my own cooking to save money. And I'm very surprised at just how much I have saved too. But you're not to worry about my finances any more. I got a decent redundancy and I'll still get some money every month from Fantasy Adventure and . . .' his voice rose a little, 'I had a call yesterday from Jimmy Craig. He's got a friend who's looking for an experienced salesman.'

'And they don't come much more experienced than you,' I said.

Dad laughed again. 'He's invited me in for an informal chat. That's all it is at this stage. But when I go in there with my new haircut,' he winked at Claire, 'well, who knows?' Then, in a much more serious voice, he said, 'I am very grateful to you both.'

'Don't bother about being grateful, Dad,' I replied. 'Just promise that whatever happens in the future you won't pull that disappearing act on us again.'

Dad looked at Claire and me, both staring intently at him and said firmly, 'That's a promise.'

Chapter Nineteen

Dad had half-guessed what Claire and me had been up to. We certainly did want to get him back on his feet and working again. What he didn't realize is that we had much bigger plans for him than that. We were going to get him back with his wife as well.

And the day when that happened was fast approaching. In fact, Claire and I were soon pressing forward with the final part of DM2.

First of all, I asked Dad if I could have my birthday party at his house.

'Of course you can,' he replied. 'Just tell me how many friends you're inviting – and try not to scare me too much.'

'Actually, I want it to be just a family occasion.' Then in case he needed reminding who exactly I meant by that, I said, 'So that's you, me, Claire and . . . Mum.'

Dad swallowed hard a couple of times and said, 'If that's what you want – fine.'

Later in the week, I popped round to Mum's house to fill her in on the party plans. She'd already assumed I'd be having the party at her house.

'But I thought you were coming home on your birthday.'

'I am, straight after the party at Dad's pad.'

'I see. And your father knows I shall be . . .'

'Yeah, and he's chuffed to bits about it.'

Mum looked as if she didn't quite believe me. She went very quiet for a moment before saying, 'Well, I'll make the cake anyhow and I expect you'd like me to bring along some other food too.'

I was about to say, 'No, Dad's going to cook a meal,' but then I decided no, let that be a major surprise for Mum.

I also decided that it would be good to have one other guest at my party: Lee. After all, he'd helped me a lot over the past weeks. I felt he deserved to be there. And Claire agreed.

So Lee was all set to come along, but at the last minute he heard his dad was zooming over to visit him on the 18th.

'Is he bringing Eileen with him?'

'He wanted to, but Mum said she wouldn't have

that woman in her house. So he's coming alone.'

'Well, bring him to my party too.'

Lee considered. 'I think it might be a bit distracting with my dad popping up after all this time. No, it's best if I don't come along . . . I'll want a full update afterwards, though.'

'You'll get it,' I said. 'It's going to be an epic night.'

Everything was going so well until Saturday afternoon . . . the last Saturday before my birthday.

Quite out of the blue, Mum asked, 'Joe, as an extra treat, how would you like to go to a film première on the day before your birthday? I can get a ticket for Claire too.'

'I'd like it very much. What's the film?'

'I'm not sure. I know Jim Carrey is in it and it's a comedy.'

'That's enough, we'll go, won't we?' I said, turning to Claire.

She nodded excitedly. 'I've never been to a film première before.'

'Neither have I. Shocking really, that someone like me, who's as cool as an ice cube, hasn't been invited before . . .'

'What's even more shocking,' interrupted Mum, 'is that I've never gone to a film première either.'

'So how did you get tickets for this one?' I asked.

'Well, actually,' replied Mum, 'these tickets belong to Roger.'

'Roger!' I cried. You'd have thought there would have been some kind of warning when he was about to reappear in your life, wouldn't you? Like a bolt of lightning, or dogs forming into packs outside your house and howling loudly.

I felt like howling myself. Roger. I thought those plastic flowers had scuppered his chances with Mum for ever. But no, here he was trying to sneak his way into our lives again.

And had Mum blushed when she said his name? I hoped not, as I knew that was a very, very bad sign.

Mum, seeing our horrified faces added hastily, 'Roger can't come with us. He'll be abroad on business, but he knows it's your birthday next Friday.'

'How does he know?' I demanded.

'I must have told him.'

'But Mum, that's private,' I said.

'Oh, don't be silly, love. I think it came up in conversation, and then he mentioned how he had these tickets which he couldn't use himself . . .'

'And neither can we,' I interrupted. Then I looked at Claire for back-up.

'No, we can't,' she said at once.

'Oh, for goodness' sake,' began Mum. 'You're both being . . .' but then she saw our determined faces and said, 'Well, you're the ones missing out. I think it would have been a super treat.'

I dare say she was right. But there was no way we could ever accept a bribe from Roger, and that's what those tickets were. It was all part of his clever ploy to win us round – and of course, to impress Mum too.

For the rest of that day, Mum wasn't exactly cross with us but she was certainly quiet and thoughtful. I started wondering how much she liked Roger. Surely she couldn't fancy him. That idea was too gruesome for words.

No, Mum was just a little impressed by his importance in the company – and by the way he splashed his money around.

Roger would try again though. That was as predictable as gravity. I just never expected it to be quite so soon.

The following Tuesday, to be precise. It was five o'clock and I was just shooting off to see Denise and get something for tea (mushroom omelette tonight) when the phone rang.

'Joe, it's me,' said Claire, in such a doom-laden voice that I knew straightaway something was very wrong.

'I'm going to talk fast because Mum's only at the front door chatting to someone. There's a message on the answerphone from Roger. I've just played it. He says he's going to Germany for a few days but he'll be back on Friday and he's got a present for you.'

'Oh, what!'

'It gets worse. He knows there's a birthday party for you at Dad's house and wondered if he could drop in and deliver the present personally.'

'No!' I cried. 'We can't have him wandering in just as Mum and Dad are reconciling. He could sabotage the whole thing.'

'I know!' shrieked Claire. 'The thing is, he says he's forgotten the house number and wants Mum to ring him back with the full address before seven o'clock, as he's leaving for Germany then for two days. So what are we going to do?'

'Mum hasn't heard the message, has she?'

'No.'

'Wipe it off then.'

'I've done that already.'

'Oh,' I said, a bit surprised. 'Well done. The next thing is to switch Mum's mobile off. He might try and call her on there.'

'Mum's already switched it off. I've checked. I think that's why he rang our home number.'

'Good. Well, every time the phone rings you must answer it.'

'But if he calls again,' her voice rose, 'what on earth am I going to say to him?'

'We could say we've switched the day,' I began.

'Yes,' agreed Claire. 'But would he believe that? We don't want him ringing up Mum to check. Shall I just give him the wrong address?'

'The trouble is, he won't stay long at the wrong address, will he? And he knows which road Dad lives in.'

Claire sighed heavily. 'We wanted Friday to be perfect, didn't we, and now it's all spoilt.'

'No, it isn't. We'll outwit Roger yet, and if we just keep him away on Friday . . . well it won't matter after that. I mean, once Mum sees Dad all dressed up and tastes his cooking, Roger will instantly fade from her memory.'

Then Claire hissed, 'I think Mum's coming back in. Yes, she is.'

'I'll think of something if it kills me. And I'll ring you back soon.'

'All right, but hurry, Joe.'

The phone clicked off. I started stomping around the room. I can usually think better when I'm walking about. But that day I drew a total blank.

Then Dad came back and began chatting away

to me. And I couldn't think at all. In the end I said I was off to the shop to get tonight's ingredients.

I wandered into the shop and waited while Denise served another customer, still desperately trying to come up with an idea. Then Denise beamed at me. 'Hello Joe, what's it tonight then?'

'Oh, just mushrooms and eggs,' I said.

I gave Denise the money and she looked at me anxiously. 'Anything wrong? You don't look your usual cheerful self.'

I forced a smile. 'No, I'm fine.'

'Thinking about your birthday on Friday, are you?'

I nodded. And that was the truth.

'Are you having the party at your house?'

'Yes, I am,' I said, vaguely.

'I only asked because we've had a last minute cancellation for one of the rooms at the Leisure Centre on Friday. So I thought if you wanted a bit more space you could use that. Also, the trouble with having a party in a house is you can have so many breakages, as I know from my son's sixteenth . . .'

Denise went on talking but I'd stopped listening, for an idea had just exploded in my head like a firework. All at once I knew what to do about Roger. I felt like shouting out, 'Eureka, Eureka.' Instead, I cried, 'Denise, you're a real life-saver because I do need somewhere to hold my party and the Leisure Centre would be ideal. Could you book it up for me rightaway before anyone else gets it?'

'Of course I can, love.' She got out a little pad. 'Now, what time would you need it from?'

'Five o'clock.'

'That's fine,' she said, writing it down, 'And how long will you want the room for?'

'Half an hour. An hour at the most.'

'Is that all?' she exclaimed.

'Yes, it's a fairly short party as people can't stay long.'

'Oh dear. Well, I'll book it for two hours anyway. And I'll get someone to cover for me here so that I can be there too.'

'Excellent. Anyway, I've got to make an urgent phone call now. See you soon.'

I sprinted back to my house, practically threw the ingredients at Dad, saying, 'Will you start the meal tonight? I've got to ring someone about . . . about my homework.'

'Now, that's a first, isn't it?' laughed Dad.

I laughed too, switched the radio in the kitchen right up, then dived to the phone.

Claire answered it at once.

'Is Mum around?' I asked.

'Yes, she is.'

'Just listen then. I want you to ring up Roger when Mum's not listening and be as sweet and nice as you can. Tell him that Mum's had to go out and that's why you're ringing him, OK?'

'OK,' whispered Claire.

'Then you will say that the party is not at Dad's house but at the Leisure Centre, just up the road. And it starts promptly at five o'clock.'

'But why am I telling him that?' she hissed.

'Because this year, I'm having two birthday parties.'

Chapter Twenty

'So if you've got any spare cakes at all, Denise, that would be brilliant.'

It was the next day and I'd invited Denise round for a cup of tea on her way to work. I knew my dad would be staying on late at Fantasy Adventure (stocktaking) so I could chat with her about my other party, undisturbed.

'Of course I'll make some cakes for you, tomorrow,' said Denise. 'And what about a birthday cake?'

'We haven't got round to that yet,' I murmured.

'Well, leave that to me.'

'Are you sure?'

'Yes, it'll be a pleasure to do some baking for someone again. Any sort of cake?'

'No, whatever you want – and it hasn't got to be very big.' I felt guilty that she was going to all this trouble for what was just a spoof party, really.

'There is one more thing,' I said. 'We're not sure how many people we've got coming to this party.' In fact, I knew exactly how many: four. There'd be Roger and me. Plus, I'd told Lee what I was up to. So he was going to swell the ranks by turning up with his dad. 'And there may not be huge numbers,' I continued. 'So I wondered if any of the staff at the Leisure Centre would like to drop in? And maybe some people from the classes too.'

'I'm sure they'd love to,' said Denise. 'But your mum and dad won't mind all these strangers invading?'

'No, they won't mind.'

'Well, I'll put the word around. I must say I'm really looking forward to meeting your mum and Claire . . . and seeing your dad again.'

Of course Denise wasn't actually going to be seeing any of them on Friday. I had to prepare her.

'By the way, I'm not sure if my mum will be able to come.'

'Oh dear, why not?' exclaimed Denise.

'She's kind of busy at work. If she can get away she will but she's not sure. And my dad will be late too: he's tidying up at Fantasy Adventure. You know how it is.'

'Yes,' she murmured. But she looked devastated on my behalf. Then she leaned forward and patted my hand. 'We'll make it a party to remember anyway.'

And she went on looking at me in this sad, pitying way until finally I couldn't stand it. I had to slip her the real lowdown on this party.

'Actually, Denise, and this is a bit of a secret, I'll be having two birthday parties on Friday. One will be at my house and that's the important one, because my mum and dad are going to be there. It's the first time Mum will have seen Dad in yonks. And he's going to cook her a special meal.'

'Oh, lovely. So they're talking again.'

'On Friday they will be, yes.'

'I see,' said Denise, in a slightly dazed way.

'Claire and I also think they're going to get back together because Dad's completely transformed himself. Mum's not going to believe her eyes.'

'It sounds as if it's going to be quite a party,' said Denise.

'The best.'

'So your other party – the one at the Leisure Centre . . .'

'That's not a real party – it's just a fake, but it's got to seem real to put Roger off the scent.'

'Now I'm lost.'

'Sorry. Let me explain. Roger's this guy who's been sniffing around Mum for ages. He's got all the personality of a cricket bat and is about as attractive as a dead pig. But he's got lots of money and he's very . . . persistent.'

'I see.'

'Would you believe he's even invited himself to my party? Now, the last thing we want is him turning up at Dad's house. That would be a twenty-four carat disaster, wouldn't it?'

Denise smiled and nodded.

'So instead, we're going to send Roger to another party . . . at the Leisure Centre. Then he'll be safely out of the way while Mum and Dad are reconciling. You gave me the idea, actually.'

'I did?'

'Yeah, that day in the shop when you asked me if I wanted to borrow the Leisure Centre for my birthday. So thanks a million for that.'

'That's all right,' she said, faintly.

'Now, we've booked the party for five o'clock, haven't we?'

Denise nodded.

'So what will happen is: Roger'll arrive at the Leisure Centre, thinking the party's there. I'll

166

meet him and take him inside. And of course we want him to think he's at the real party. That's why everything must seem authentic.

'But he's not exactly a party animal. I mean, I bet he'll turn up in his suit and will just sit in the corner reading the *Financial Times*, waiting for my mum. Who, of course, will never turn up.'

'Won't he think that's a little odd?' asked Denise.

'Ah well, I've got a plan for that.' I smiled shyly. 'It involves you, actually. Could you come up to me at half past five and say in front of Roger, "Your mum's just rung to say she's been badly delayed in traffic and won't be here in time, so go ahead and cut the cake without her." So we'll cut the cake and then Roger, who's only there really to see Mum, will slink off, and I'll charge back to my real party and . . .'

I stopped. 'You're looking a bit uncertain, Denise.'

'No, no . . .'

'Look, if you don't want to say all that to Roger . . .'

'It's not that I don't want to. It's just . . . well it's rather difficult for me. I can't really be seen to be meddling in your parents' lives.'

'I totally understand.' Then, after a slight

pause, 'Will you still be able to make the cakes, though?'

'Oh yes, leave all the catering to me,' she said.

'That's a huge help, thanks. And don't worry about Roger. I'll go and tell him Mum's been delayed. He'll believe me as I've got an honest face, haven't I?'

Denise smiled. 'Now, that's exactly what Paul used to say to me. And he was always up to some mischief too.' Then she glanced at her watch and jumped up. 'I must fly. But don't worry, I'll make a nice cake and I hope everything works out for you on Friday.'

She made as if to go, then turned round again. 'May I give you one piece of advice?'

'Sure.'

'Just remember, Joe, adults don't always move as fast as you'd like them to. In fact, sometimes they move very slowly.' She smiled. 'But usually they get there in the end.'

'I know what you're saying,' I replied. 'But you see, Mum and Dad only separated because of Dad's bad habits. And now he hasn't got any. Claire and I have got rid of them all . . . and when Mum finds out it's going to be just incredible.'

Chapter Twenty-one

Now, I wouldn't pretend it was the party of the year or anything like that. But if you happened to be passing my local Leisure Centre on Friday at around twenty past five and looked in, you'd have seen a room packed with people of all ages, talking, laughing and even dancing a few steps (two intrepid ladies from the Knitting Club). Meanwhile, the Keep Fit Club were shoulder to shoulder around the food.

This was set out on a long table at the end of the room. There were plates of cakes and biscuits as well as sausage rolls, crisps and nuts and jugs of orange and lemonade. While bang in the centre was a huge birthday cake with 'Happy Birthday Joe' in blue icing on it. Denise must have been up all night baking this: it really set the table off.

There was one surprise – no sign of Lee and his

169

dad. But everyone else had arrived including . . .
yes, Roger was here all right. He blew in on the
dot of five o'clock.

Now he was wandering around the edges of the
party with a beaker of orange juice in one hand
and a cake in the other. He was wearing his grey
suit, but he had taken off his tie and he wasn't
reading the *Financial Times* either. Instead, he
was tapping a toe and sort of nodding along to
the music as if to prove he was a bit of a groover
really.

I'd been doing a spot of mingling with 'my
guests' when he signalled me to come over. I took
a quick squint at my watch. It was twenty-two
minutes past five. Just eight minutes to go before
the cake cutting and the end of this party.

'That song they're playing,' Roger asked me.
'Is it in the charts?'

'It was, about twenty-five years ago.'

'Oh, it's quite catchy and I just wondered . . .'
his voice fell away but quickly started up again.
'There's certainly a real mixture of people here
and they all seem to be having an enjoyable time.
I'm very grateful that you've allowed me to be
part of this special evening.' He smiled broadly.
All his teeth sprung out and he looked like a
Derby winner.

He was also being disgustingly creepy, which

meant he must like Mum a lot. That thought alarmed me. The sooner Mum and Dad were safely back together the better.

'But no sign of your mother yet,' he said.

'No, not yet.'

'Anyway, I'd like to give you my little present now. It's nothing very exciting, I'm afraid.'

And it wasn't. It was a set of pens.

'You can never have too many pens, can you?' said Roger.

'No,' I murmured. I felt obliged to add. 'Thanks.' Then I went on, 'But you shouldn't waste your money on someone you hardly know.'

'Sorry, what was that?' said Roger. 'The music's rather loud, making it difficult to hear properly.' He leaned forward.

'I said you shouldn't waste your money on someone you hardly know.'

Roger moved even closer to me. There were little beads of sweat all over his forehead. 'Well,' he said, 'I hope in time we can become . . . friends.'

I didn't answer, just looked a bit sick.

'And if ever you wanted to talk to me, or ask me about anything.'

I shuddered at the very idea. 'Like what?' I asked.

He hesitated. 'Well, er . . .'

'About girls and stuff, do you mean?'

A look of total horror crossed his face. 'Oh no, no, no. Just general advice.'

'My dad gives me all the advice I'll ever need, thanks.' I must have said that pretty forcefully because he stepped back from me and didn't say anything else. Then he plonked himself down on one of the canvas chairs by the table.

He looked more than a bit shaken and was shifting about on the chair as if he had ants in his pants. I thought, any moment now he will leap up and stalk off home. I kept hoping he'd do that. But he didn't.

So at half past five I walked over to Roger again. And I was just about to deliver Mum's imaginary message – when Denise got in before me. She rushed up, saying, 'Oh Joe, we've just had a message from your mum. She's been delayed in a most horrendous traffic jam and she said to go ahead and cut the cake without her.'

'Did she say when she expects to get here?' asked Roger anxiously.

'No, but it might be some time yet. She's very upset about it, but there we are . . . still, your dad will be here soon, won't he?'

'Oh yes, any minute now,' I said.

Roger shifted uncomfortably. Denise moved away.

'Thanks so much for saying that,' I hissed. 'It had much more cred coming from you.'

'Well, to be honest, love, he looked so uncomfortable sitting there, I thought I might as well put him out of his misery.'

Then the music was switched off, the lights dimmed, and there was a great roar of 'Happy Birthday' followed by the cutting of the birthday cake.

Now, when people cut the cake that's like the end credits on a film, isn't it? A sure sign the party's over. And after they'd wolfed down their piece of cake people did start to move off.

But not Roger. He wasn't even pretending to have a good time now. Instead, he sat on that chair with a grimly determined look on his face, like someone who's going to wait for a train no matter how late it comes in.

And time was rushing on until suddenly it was five to six. Mum would be arriving any moment now. I wanted to be there when she first saw Dad. Instead, I was missing it because I was stuck here with my worst enemy, Roger.

Denise came over to me.

'Why won't he go home?' I whispered.

She smiled sympathetically.

'I bet everyone else will leave,' I cried, 'and he'll be the last guest left.'

She patted my hand, 'Do you want to slip off home for a few minutes, love?'

'Are you sure?'

'Yes,' she whispered. 'I'll cover for you. Come back in about twenty minutes though. And if he hasn't gone then . . .'

'We'll just have to carry him out, chair and all,' I said.

I sneaked out of the door and then bolted up the road. I don't know what the record is for running between the Leisure Centre and my house but I wouldn't be a bit surprised if I hold it now. And thanks to all those times I'd gone running with Dad I wasn't out of breath – well, not much anyhow.

Claire was waiting at the door for me. 'Has Roger gone?' she asked hopefully.

'Not quite. I've got to slip back in about twenty minutes.'

'Oh no.'

'Don't worry, it'll sort itself out. Much more important: how are things here? I bet Mum got the shock of her life when she saw Dad.'

'Oh she did,' said Claire eagerly. 'And she keeps sneaking these little looks at him as if she can't believe her eyes.'

'Excellent.'

'But she hasn't said much. Neither has Dad.

But they're being very polite to each other.'

We went into the sitting room. Mum was looking out of the window. She whirled round. 'At last, here he is, the birthday boy.'

Then Dad came in with a tray of tea and biscuits and I just felt so proud. There he was, in his light blue Ralph Lauren shirt, pleated-front trousers and loafers. Not to mention his sharp new haircut. I tell you, he looked the business. And he put the tray down so suavely, then started handing round the teas as if he'd done it all his life.

There was just one sofa in the sitting room, so Mum and Dad sat on that, while Claire and I got a couple of chairs from the kitchen.

When we returned Mum had already started sipping her tea. Claire and I watched her.

'How's your tea?' I asked.

'It's just fine.' Then after a pause, she said to Dad, 'Well, I'm glad the weather's kept nice for Joe's birthday. It had clouded over earlier, hadn't it?'

'So it had,' agreed Dad. 'And it was very cold for July yesterday, wasn't it?'

They were both searching for things to say to each other. And although they were chatting, their eyes never actually met. They sat staring ahead like two newsreaders.

Their conversation was going absolutely nowhere. It was up to Claire and me to move things along. I gave her a look. Claire immediately picked up my cue.

'This sitting room is so neat and clean, isn't it Mum?' she said.

'Yes, it is.' She gave a little smile. 'I must say I'm quite surprised.'

'Are you?' I began. 'Well, you want to see upstairs.'

'Oh yes,' agreed Claire. 'Why don't we go and see it now?'

'Let your mother finish her tea first,' said Dad.

But I didn't have time to waste. 'Bring your tea with you, Mum. We'll give you a tour.'

'There's nothing to see really,' protested Dad. But Claire and I were already surging up the stairs. So Mum had no choice but to follow us, with Dad bringing up the rear.

'We'll start with the bathroom,' I suggested, as Dad had worked especially hard here. We all crowded inside. 'First of all, Mum, look at those chrome taps, don't they just shine and gleam?'

'Well, yes,' admitted Mum, 'they do.'

'And this sink,' cried Claire, peering down into it. 'Look Mum, it's absolutely spotless.' Mum had a peek. And I saw her noticing the brand new bar of soap there too.

'Now observe the bath, Mum. Go on, get down and have a proper look,' I continued.

Mum crouched down and gazed into the bath. She was dead fascinated. I could tell.

'Now what do you see,' I said, 'or rather don't see: no tide marks are there? And you hate those, don't you?'

'Well, er . . .' began Mum.

'All right, you two,' grinned Dad. 'You sound like estate agents.'

Mum finished scrutinizing the bath and stood up. 'No, I must say I'm very impressed by how very clean everything is.' And for the first time, Mum actually looked at Dad. It was only for a micro second. But Claire and I still exchanged glances.

'Next on the tour guide schedule is my room,' I said. 'Notice how Dad insists I keep this room tidy. He runs a very tight ship.' I saw Mum having a good look round, her gaze lingered on my cases all packed in the corner and ready for me to leave with her tonight. And again she stole a glance at Dad.

'I can see you've been looked after very well.'

'And did you know,' I cried, 'Dad dusts this room practically every day.'

He began to protest. 'Oh, I don't know about that.'

'You're being too modest, Dad. Look, Mum, come and run your finger along the window sill.'

She hesitated.

'Just ignore him,' grinned Dad.

'No, go on, Mum,' urged Claire. 'Please.'

Smiling now, in an embarrassed way, Mum ran her finger along the window sill.

'Now look at your finger,' I said. 'Do you see any dust? Do you?'

At that moment the strangest thing happened. Mum suddenly broke into great peals of laughter. She put her head back and really laughed. Only she was laughing so much, she was crying too.

She wasn't the only one. Dad was cracking up as well, while Claire and I watched them both in surprise. What was so amusing? I didn't get it. But still, the important thing was, they were laughing, and laughing together too.

'Oh Joe, you're so funny,' began Mum, wiping her eyes.

'I'm afraid he takes after me,' laughed Dad.

'Yes,' replied Mum, 'I think he does.' And they were gazing right at each other now.

'Now would you like another cup of tea?' asked Dad.

'That would be lovely,' said Mum, still wiping her eyes.

I was about to point out that we hadn't been to Dad's room yet, but then I figured maybe it was better that way.

Mum and Dad walked downstairs together chatting away – and not about the weather either.

'Did you see that?' whispered Claire. 'It's really happening.'

'I know. Just magic to watch, isn't it?'

Everything was going perfectly until I looked at my watch. Twenty past six. I murmured to Claire, 'I've got to slip back. I won't be long.'

Then I opened my bedroom window and called out to no-one in particular. 'OK, Lee, I'll be right down.'

I went into the sitting room. Mum and Dad were still nattering away and the atmosphere was so easy and natural I felt I would burst with happiness. 'That was Lee outside,' I told them. 'He's got a present for me but doesn't want to come in.'

'Why ever not?' asked Mum.

'He doesn't want to intrude on a family occasion. So I'll just shoot out and see him.'

'Well, don't be long, love,' said Mum. 'We haven't even cut your cake yet.'

I tore off down the road again. Only this time

with a massive smile on my face which I just couldn't lose.

The smile only fell away when I got back to the Leisure Centre. The party was really thinning out now but Roger was still there. Only now he'd put on his horn-rimmed glasses and was sitting behind the table.

'I can't believe he's still here,' I whispered to Denise.

'I've a feeling, love,' she said, 'he's not going to budge until he's seen your mother.'

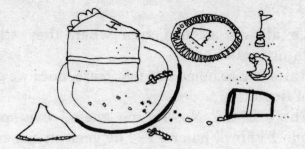

Chapter Twenty-two

I started walking towards Roger, wishing with every molecule in my body I could get him to leave. Maybe I should just tell him the party's finished. But he still might hang around, perhaps even offer to help clear up, in the hope of sighting Mum.

And he had to go now.

I was still on my way over to him when Lee rushed up. 'I'm really sorry, mate. We got held up in this almighty traffic jam . . .'

'Don't worry about it. Is your dad coming in?'

'Yeah, he's just parking the car.'

'Well, I just nipped home for a bit. And would you believe, I left my mum and dad chewing the cud together.'

'That's excellent news.'

'It was so weird. They were looking around the house when they both just burst out laughing.'

'It's always a good sign when they start laughing,' said Lee.

'I think we're home and dry, mate, once we get rid of Roger.'

'Where is he? No, let me guess.' Lee spun round. 'I know!' he cried. 'The geek in the suit sitting down. It's got to be him.'

'In the flesh.'

Before I could say any more, an enormous hand landed on my shoulder. I looked up to see fifteen stone of Lee's dad grinning at me. He'd played rugby professionally in his heyday and looked as if he still could now. He was a huge guy with hundreds of freckles on his face and carroty hair.

He and I had always got on quite well in the past, and he seemed genuinely pleased to see me now. He kept patting me on the shoulder and laughing heartily. And then I noticed how Roger was watching us very keenly, even standing up as if to get a better view at one point.

Finally, Lee's dad lumbered off to see if there was any birthday cake left. And straightaway, Roger began moving towards us at a smartish pace. I nudged Lee and then Roger was saying, 'Ah, here you are, Joe. I was afraid we'd lost you.'

I wish we could lose you, I thought.

Roger went on. 'The gentleman you were just talking to . . . I assume that was your father.'

I was about to say no when I noticed how very apprehensive Roger was looking. So my brain gave itself a little shake and I said, 'Yes, you're right. That's my dad.'

Lee's jaw dropped to the floor with shock. I quickly continued, 'And when I told him you were here he wasn't the least bit happy.'

'Wasn't he?' quavered Roger, sneaking a glance across the room at the enormous bulk of Lee's dad.

'No, he was furious, actually, said you had no right to be here.'

Lee, quickly realizing what I was doing joined in. 'And I wouldn't want to get on the wrong side of your dad, Joe. He's got a ferocious temper, hasn't he?'

'Oh, but he's nowhere near as bad as he used to be,' I said.

Roger's nose was quivering like a rabbit's now.

'Watch out, I think he's coming back,' cried Lee. 'Yes, he is.'

'Well, in the light of his attitude to me, it might perhaps be wise if I left now,' said Roger, in a low voice.

'I think it would, actually,' I said, trying hard to keep the eagerness out of my voice. 'Thanks for the pens and . . . well you know the way out, don't you.'

'Yes I do . . . a hasty goodbye then, and tell your mother I was here, won't you?' With a brisk wave, Roger was off. At last, he was really going.

Before I could say anything to Lee, his dad had returned brandishing two plates of cake.

'Mmm, it's delicious,' he said. 'Tuck in, Lee.'

'I'm glad you like it,' I began. 'I . . .' But then my voice trailed away because I'd just seen something truly awful.

Roger was coming back. He was making straight for us too. Lee and I exchanged looks. What could we do? There was no time even to think. For the next moment, Roger was squinting up at Lee's dad and saying, 'I just wanted you to know I didn't come here to cause any unpleasantness.'

Lee's dad looked totally bewildered, and who could blame him. 'Just who are you?' he cried, spraying Roger with crumbs of cake as he did so.

'I'm . . .' Roger swallowed hard, 'I'm a friend of your wife's. I'm . . .'

'Oh, yes,' interrupted Lee's dad. 'I know all about you.'

'You do?'

'My son's mentioned you quite a lot.'

'Ah, good,' murmured Roger.

The two men stared at each other. They both looked suddenly embarrassed, while Lee and I were desperately thinking how we could end this conversation before it went totally pear-shaped.

'I just thought we should meet,' said Roger. 'And I wanted to explain . . .'

'There's nothing to explain. My wife is free to see who she wants.'

'Really!' exclaimed Roger.

'Well, I'd be a hypocrite if I raised any objections. You see, I have a lady friend myself. Her name's Eileen and it's serious, actually. I'm surprised my wife hasn't mentioned her.'

'Well, anyway, it's great you two have met now,' I interrupted.

'And you are getting on so well too,' chipped in Lee.

'If you treat my son right, you won't get any objections from me,' said Lee's dad, stretching out an enormous hand to Roger.

The two shook hands. Roger couldn't help wincing. Lee's dad had a grip of steel. Then Lee's dad turned to me and boomed, 'I know your mother's been held up in traffic but I don't see your father anywhere. Is he here?'

My heart actually turned a double somersault. I swear it did. But amazingly, incredibly, Roger didn't react. Then I noticed what I can only describe as a look of elation plastered across Roger's face. The news of my 'dad's' girlfriend had cheered him up so much he'd gone into a kind of trance.

So I murmured to Lee's father, 'Yes, my dad's around.'

'Oh well, perhaps I'll see him later. Now, I'm off to see if I can get any more of that delicious cake.'

He ambled off while I hissed to Lee, 'Thanks a million, mate.'

'Oh, any time you want to borrow my dad, just let me know,' he grinned. Then he wiped his forehead as if to say that was a close shave. And it really had been.

Roger was still tottering about like a man in a dream. Time to get him off the premises once and for all, before anything else happened.

'Shall I see you out?' I asked him, in my politest voice.

'Oh, how kind of you,' said Roger. Kindness had nothing to do with it. I wanted to make sure he really left this time.

Along the way I caught Denise's eye. I whispered to her, 'As soon as he's out of the door, the party's over.'

She nodded, then hissed, 'And you cut off back home. I can clear up here.'

'Are you sure?'

'Yes, it won't take long. How's it going at home?'

'It couldn't be better.'

She gave me the thumbs-up and then I followed Roger out of the door.

Of course there would be repercussions from this little deception later. But by then Mum and Dad would be safely back together. They might even marvel at Claire's and my ingenuity. I was imagining this happy scene when I heard a very familiar voice calling my name. And then she said Roger's name too.

I thought, this is a momentary hallucination caused by too much stress. My mum isn't really charging towards me. I shall rub my eyes and she will be gone.

I even gave my eyes a little rub just to check, but I'm afraid she didn't disappear. In fact, she loomed up closer and closer.

Afterwards, Claire explained that Mum had grown impatient waiting for me. She'd said it was silly for Lee to skulk outside. He was practically one of the family anyway. So Mum charged off to invite Lee inside to have some cake. Claire felt bad she hadn't managed to stop Mum. But there was nothing she could have done. When Mum decides to do something, that's it.

She had followed Mum outside and when I wasn't immediately visible, she tried her best to persuade Mum to come back inside. But by then Mum was up the road and eyeballing something else. 'But that looks just like Roger's car!' she exclaimed.

And unfortunately, Mum decided to have a closer peer, just as Roger and I were leaving the party.

Roger steamed over to her. 'Ah, you've made it! There's been a terrible traffic jam, hasn't there?'

Mum gaped at him, her eyes widening alarmingly. 'What . . . ?'

'Anyway, I mustn't keep you talking out here,' said Roger. 'You'll want to catch the last moments of Joe's birthday party.' Then he leaned forward confidingly. 'Your husband's inside there by the way.'

If Roger had started babbling in Greek I don't think Mum could have looked more astonished. She turned to me. I tried to smile at her in a reassuring manner.

'You think my husband's in there?' she cried.

'Oh, I can assure you he is, but don't worry, we had a very civilized conversation and he told me about Eileen . . .'

'Eileen?' squawked Mum.

Roger was staring at her in some alarm now.

'I'm sorry, I'm being very indelicate.' He began to back away. 'Look, I will ring you tomorrow if I may. Goodbye for now.'

He dived into his car and drove away.

Claire and I were doing our best to melt away too. But Mum wasn't having any of it.

'You two!' she called. 'Will you kindly tell me what on earth is going on?'

'What do you mean?' I asked, trying to sound innocent and missing by a mile.

'I mean, why have you got a birthday party going on in the Leisure Centre? What was Roger doing at it? And why does he think he's just been talking to your father? And, oh yes – who on earth is Eileen?'

There was, what you might call, a sticky silence for several moments. Then I took a good long breath and said, 'Now which question would you like me to answer first, Mum?'

Chapter Twenty-three

The next half hour was pretty ghastly. The four of us were in the sitting room. Dad not saying much and Mum saying plenty. I tell you, she was madder than a bag full of ferrets.

'Now let me get this straight,' she said, her blue eyes flashing, 'because I'm finding it very hard to understand.' Mum paused to direct the full beam of her anger at me. Claire, perhaps wisely, was examining her hands.

'You didn't want Roger to come round here with the present he'd got for your birthday, so you play this practical joke on him?'

'No, it wasn't a practical joke,' I insisted.

'What was it then?' she demanded.

'It was just . . . we didn't want him round at Dad's, so we made up somewhere else for him to go instead.'

'But why? What has this poor man done to you to inspire such hatred?'

'We don't exactly hate him,' I began. 'We just didn't want him round here today.'

'Oh, for goodness' sake,' sighed Mum. 'Imagine if I took that attitude to all your friends every time they popped up. Well, you're going to have to apologize to him.'

'All right. No sweat. But he did enjoy himself. I mean that's why I had to pretend about Lee's dad . . . it was the only way I could get him to leave.'

'That's not the point,' said Mum.

'Yes, it is. You're acting as if we tied him up and hid him under the floorboards or something . . . He went to a party, Mum.'

'I must say,' said Dad, breaking into the interrogation for the first time, 'I feel rather at a loss in all this, never having met Roger or even known of his existence until tonight.' Then he gave a strange laugh: the kind of laugh you give when you're not really amused. Mum gave him her frowniest look. He turned to me. 'You must have spent hours preparing this fake party.'

'We did,' I muttered.

'And no adults helped you to book the room or prepare the food?' asked Mum.

'Not especially,' I murmured. I thought it would be best to keep Denise out of this mess. 'It was certainly all our own idea.'

'Well, it's been a lot of silliness and confusion for nothing,' continued Mum. 'Why couldn't you just have come to me and said you didn't want Roger here today?'

I hesitated. I mean, how do you answer a question like that without sounding snide? But then Dad answered it for me. 'Maybe they felt they couldn't tell you something like that.'

Well, that hit the spot all right. Mum actually flinched, then said in this very clipped tone. 'Thank you, thank you very much. I can always rely on you not to support me, can't I?'

'I was merely pointing out . . .' began Dad.

'I know exactly what you were doing,' snapped Mum, her voice falling lower and lower. 'You're always trying to turn the children against me, making out you're so jolly and relaxed all the time. Well, it's easy to be like that when you hand over all the responsibility to me.'

'What rubbish,' retorted Dad, in an even quieter voice. 'And I would be grateful if you would stop making nasty cracks about me in front of the children. You see, I know exactly what you've been saying . . .'

They were glowering at each other now. And a

full-blown argument could only be seconds away. No doubt they'd be retiring to the kitchen shortly to really slug it out.

And I couldn't believe how easily my mum and dad had slipped back into their bad old ways. They'd been getting on so well too, but now they were just throwing it all away again. I was so angry with them and I was about to say something when Claire suddenly raised her head and wailed, 'You were nice to each other for a few minutes but now you're going back to how you were before. And I'm just sick of it.'

She sprang up and ran to the door. I thought she was going to run upstairs but instead she spun round and shouted, 'Do you know what the last few months have been like for Joe and me? Do you?'

I think Mum and Dad were both too stunned to answer. 'First of all Joe and I just felt so guilty, as if you and Dad breaking up was somehow our fault.' Mum tried to interrupt here but Claire just stormed on. 'It was bad enough when we had to run between the pair of you and we felt as if we were split in two all the time. But it was much worse when you stopped talking to each other. I mean, how childish is that?

'Actually, I think you're both acting like big children!' She wagged her finger at Mum and

Dad. 'I can't believe you've gone on not talking to each other for all these months.

'And now if I even mention Dad's name, Mum, you go all funny. And if I tell you that Dad's bought me something you're mad about it for hours. And Dad, if I say Mum's name to you, you just stare at me and pretend you haven't heard anything. Then you change the subject. Well I think that's so . . .' her whole body shook with anger, 'so totally pathetic!' she practically shrieked.

'But, Claire,' began Mum.

'I haven't finished!' blazed Claire. 'Then, Dad, you just disappeared out of our lives. You stopped coming round, you never even bothered to call us. And first I made excuses for you. I thought you were just very busy. But then more weeks went past and I'd hear people at school saying, "My dad's done this and my dad does that." And I'd think, I don't know what my dad's doing any more.' Her mouth quivered for a moment. 'And in the end Joe had to go and find you in your shop. We knew something was wrong. And we wanted your help so badly, Mum, only you couldn't bear to even hear Dad's name. So we tried to help him ourselves.

'Meanwhile, Mum, you were busy bringing this weird stranger into our house. And yes, he

194

thought he could butter us up with money and stuff. But he's got nothing to do with us. And actually, Mum, it's not really the same as me bringing a schoolfriend home, because Roger could be living in the house every day with us.'

'Oh, no,' protested Mum.

'Yes he could, and he might start bossing us around too, and there's not a thing we can do about it. We don't have a vote in any of this.

'But we still wanted to help you both and get our home back to the way it was before. And maybe some of the things we did were a bit under-hand, but it was the only way we could make ourselves heard and we've tried so hard and got our hopes up. But you're just going back to arguing again. And I don't know why, because no-one gets anything out of arguments. It's just not worth it but you two . . . Oh, I just give up on you both.'

Tears were streaming down Claire's face and her knees were starting to shake too.

'Look, love,' cried Mum, making as if to go over to her.

'No, go away,' sobbed Claire furiously brushing her tears away with her sleeve. Then she looked across at me again.

In an instant I was standing beside her. I put my arm around her. I could feel her trembling.

'I'd just like to say,' I said, 'I think Claire has really hit the nail on the head, said everything that I was thinking, and all the time she was talking, I was cheering her on.'

Mum stared at us aghast. She'd gone a deathly white colour while Dad looked totally crushed. Then Claire began to blow her nose very vigorously. But I didn't flinch and kept my arm tightly around her. How many other brothers can say they'd have done the same?

Finally, Mum said in this tiny, croaky voice which didn't sound like her at all, 'Thank you for letting us know how you both feel. It's important we understand and I hadn't realized that . . . that . . .' In the end Mum's sentence just gave up on itself. 'I'm very, very sorry,' she whispered.

Then, Dad slowly got to his feet. 'You've both given us a lot to think about and I promise you we will. But first I think it might be best if I . . .' and then he hesitated as the words he was about to utter were not the ones he'd ever used before. 'How about if I go into the kitchen and see how the lamb and apple casserole is coming on? I've also prepared some jacket potatoes and a side salad. Does that sound all right?'

196

Chapter Twenty-four

Mum could only gape at Dad, speechless with shock. Then after he'd gone into the kitchen she said slowly, 'Your father did just say he is cooking us all something?'

'That's right,' I replied. 'He wanted it to be a surprise.'

'It's certainly that all right,' she gasped.

'He cooks for me every night now.'

'And for me when I come over on Sundays,' added Claire.

Mum shook her head and still looked as if she'd just seen an extraterrestrial. 'Do you know, in all the years we've been married I don't think he's so much as opened a tin!' Then she started listening to Dad working away in the kitchen. She tilted her head, completely amazed. In the end she got up and said, 'I'd better go and see if he needs a hand.'

After she'd left, I turned to Claire. 'What about that? I knew Dad cooking was our trump card!'

Moments later we heard the steady hum of Mum and Dad chatting together.

'Is there a better sound?' I said. Then I turned to Claire. 'And a lot of that is due to you. You really brought them to their senses.'

'I told them, didn't I?' Her voice began to shake again.

'I'll say.'

'I can't believe I did it now.'

'I was pretty shocked too. Nice, sweet Claire giving our parents a right tongue-lashing.'

Her eyes widened anxiously. 'You don't think I went too far?'

'No, it needed to be said. And anyway, it was good for them.'

'I really hadn't meant to say half of it,' went on Claire. 'But when they started arguing again, I got so mad and it all just tumbled out.' She leaned forward. 'They're doing a lot of talking in there, aren't they?'

'Yeah, we might be in line for a big reconciliation between them after all.'

'I think we are,' whispered Claire. 'You can just feel it in the air, can't you?'

And strangely enough, I could.

Then Dad appeared in the doorway. 'Ladies

and gentlemen, dinner is now being served.' He was wearing the most enormous chef's hat you've ever seen.

'Wherever did you get that from?' I asked.

'Oh, only top cooks are allowed to wear this you know. This hat is a sign that you are in the presence of a culinary giant.'

And there was Mum sitting at the kitchen table, chuckling at Dad's antics just as she used to. The whole situation was looking more and more hopeful.

I noticed too, how eagerly Dad was watching us all eat. But especially Mum. He kept looking at her. And when she started praising his cooking lavishly (incidentally, it was one of his very best, and for once, nothing was over-cooked) his face was one big smile.

At the end of the meal, Mum said, 'Your dad and I have just had a good talk.'

'Not before time,' I said.

'Yes, quite right,' agreed Mum. 'Now your dad has told me about losing his job.'

'But I've got an interview with a friend of a friend next week,' cut in Dad. 'And it's looking pretty good, I think.'

Mum smiled across at him, then went on. 'And your dad has also told me how you've both helped him through a very difficult time. I feel guilty that I didn't know and couldn't rally round too.'

'We did wonder about telling you,' I whispered.

'And I wish you had. But I should have known anyway. And Claire, you're quite right, parents not talking is silly and childish. And you shouldn't have to take sides or choose between us. We're both your parents and we want you to know that whatever happens, one thing will never change – and that's how much we love you.'

'In other words, you're stuck with us,' grinned Dad.

'There's something else I really should clear up.' Mum hesitated. 'It's about Roger.' She must have noticed how Claire and I tensed up because her tone became a touch defensive.

'Roger has helped me a lot at work and given me opportunities and the chance to show what I could do. And I really do think I should be entitled to bring friends home from time to time and know they will be treated with courtesy and respect.' She stopped as if waiting for Claire and me to say something, but neither of us did. We just kept our faces blank.

'Roger is a kind man and a lonely one too, I think. And he has become rather fond of me.'

'We noticed,' I murmured.

She turned to Dad as if looking for an ally. 'The

children know he sent me some roses one day, plastic ones, actually.'

Claire kicked me under the table and I couldn't look at her as I knew I'd burst out laughing.

'But the truth is,' continued Mum. Then she stopped and gave this nervous laugh. 'I feel just as if I'm in the witness box here.' Claire and I were certainly looking at her very keenly. 'The truth is, I only ever saw Roger as a friend.'

'Phew!' cried Claire.

'And double-phew from me.'

And with Roger out of the way that meant there were no obstacles to . . .

'We've something else to tell you,' said Mum, looking across at Dad now.

This was it, wasn't it. The moment Claire and I had been working for all these weeks. And right now the best thing in the world would be to hear Mum say . . .

'From now on your dad and I promise we will stay in regular communication . . .'

No, that wasn't what we wanted to hear. Well, it was OK as a starter. But what about the rest, the really, really important news? Claire and I looked at Mum. She saw our very hopeful faces, guessed what we were wanting her to say and lowered her eyes. There were spots of pink on her cheeks as she said softly, 'Your dad and I were

201

making each other unhappy living in the same house: so unhappy that we couldn't be the kind of parents you deserved. The separation was something we both needed, wasn't it?' She turned to Dad as if to confirm.

'Yes, that's right,' he said.

'And your father and I still have some things to work out,' continued Mum, a firm note in her voice suddenly. 'And you really must leave that to us now.'

'I think,' added Dad suddenly, 'your mum and I have talked more today than we have done for months and months.'

'If not years,' said Mum, with a wry smile. Then she murmured, almost apologetically, 'You see, your dad and I do need this space apart. Please try and understand that.'

There was silence after that. A pretty long silence broken by Dad saying. 'Now we've got that all sorted out, who's for birthday cake?'

I stared around me. All the colour seemed to be draining out of the room and everything was covered in this dark haze of disappointment. The cake didn't taste of anything either. Or didn't then anyhow.

I'd really thought Dad was going to come back with us. Everything seemed to point to it. What was holding them back? Dad was cooking and cleaning and he'd lost weight – what was left for them to sort out? It was all sorted, for heaven's sake.

In a kind of daze I opened my presents and then Dad was lugging my cases downstairs and it was time to go. He swept Claire up into his arms, then turned to me. 'Well, I've got my cleaning rota and I shall go on cooking for myself every night.'

'Make sure you do,' I said. 'And no lapsing into takeaways. If you need any advice, ask Denise in the shop. Go and see her anyway. She's a diamond. Give her my best and tell her I'll be in contact.'

'I will.'

'And be very careful on the motorbike, especially at night.' I lowered my voice here as I wasn't sure if Mum knew about that.

'I might be selling it soon. We'll see,' said Dad. 'I feel as if I'm at a new stage in my life now. And these last weeks . . . I'll never forget them.' He folded his long fingers around my hands and held them tightly. 'Come back soon.'

Then he picked up my cases and took them out to the car. Mum went with him and they lingered out there, talking.

Claire and I hovered in the doorway, watching them.

'I really thought they were going to . . .' began Claire.

'I know. So did I.'

We stood there in slightly dejected silence for a few moments. And suddenly into my memory bank whizzed that advice Denise had given me the day she came round here. She'd said, 'Adults don't always move as fast as you'd like them to. In fact, sometimes they move very slowly. But they get there in the end.'

I told this to Claire. 'I suppose,' I went on, 'we were a bit optimistic, thinking they were going to get back together in one evening. Adults just aren't programmed to move that fast. But look at the progress they've made today, thanks to us. They're talking again. They can't stop talking to each other now. And they're laughing . . .'

'And they're not fighting,' interrupted Claire.

'Exactly. They're really getting along. And did you see Mum's face when she was eating that lamb and apple casserole? She was thinking, I wouldn't mind someone cooking this for me on a regular basis. I tell you, we've achieved so much today.'

'Yes, I suppose you're right,' agreed Claire. 'But now Mum says we should stop.'

'And are we going to listen?' I turned to Claire. But before she could reply Mum was hustling us into the car. Still Claire didn't need to answer. That gleam in her eye told me all I needed to know.

The truth is, Claire and I won't rest until Mum and Dad are back living together again. You see, we want that more than anything else.

And yes, I know we'll have to be cleverer than before and plan our next strategy very carefully. But we'll do it all right. In my bones I just know we will.

I'll tell you something else: Mum and Dad haven't seen anything yet.

You just wait.

THE END

THE FRIGHTENERS
Pete Johnson

When Chloe starts at a new school, she gets off to a really bad start and no-one seems to want to be her friend. Except Aidan. But there's something very odd about Aidan. Everybody seems *scared* of him, and *very* scared of the pictures he draws. Chloe can't imagine why – until she picks up one of his pictures and sees a drawing of the Frighteners for the first time.

Now the Frighteners won't leave her alone . . .

A gripping tale of friendship, revenge – and an imagination that has the power to make the unreal become real.

0440 864372

THE CREEPER
Pete Johnson

Remember, you may not see me, but I shall be there . . . watching. You cannot hide from the Creeper . . .

Lucy is delighted when she spots the old audio tape in a second-hand bookshop: a spooky story, perfect for listening to at Halloween.

But then she and her friend Jack listen to the tape, and Lucy is suddenly really scared. For the story tells the terrifying tale of *the Creeper*, a horrific creature formed from the ashes of a murdered man and bent on revenge against all wrongdoers. And Lucy has just done something truly *terrible* to her best friend.

Now the Creeper is loose – and he has a new victim . . .

0440 863929